who knows
what song the
sirens sang?

WHO KNOWS WHAT SONG THE SIRENS SANG?

MYTHS REVISITED

A VOYAGE INTO THE ANTEDILUVIAN WORLD

by
Michele Buchanan, Ph.D.

The cover illustration is Odysseus/Ulysses and the Sirens, as depicted in a Greek vase painting.

 Publisher: Hummingbird Hollow Press
Albuquerque, New Mexico
www.hummingbirdhollowpress.com

ACKNOWLEDGEMENTS

Michele would like to thank the many voices that helped with this sequel to *Scota's Harp*. First, thanks to her husband Tom, who has been supremely supportive in all things, a loving *Bärenheuter*. Help also came from a long list of friends in the Wordwright Group; her editor Shari Tarbet; Dale Harris of Hummingbird Hollow Press and designer Esther Feske who brought this work into publication. And heartfelt thanks to the ancient historians without whom true history has no voice.

DEDICATION

This book is dedicated to the Celtic Singers of New Mexico,
whose singing epitomizes the songs the Sirens sang.

Author's Introduction

An elderly Irish friend once told me that his mother maintained they were "Milesians." The Irish legends being passed down to him told of a migration of their people from the Anatolian city of Miletus, many centuries BCE. Miletus was purported to be the most famous trading hub of the ancient world, having a bazaar where one could "hear over one hundred languages." According to legend, this particular clan of people migrated from the coastline city, which now lies in ruins in the country of Turkey. The legend recounts their travel to the peninsula of Spain where they "lived amongst barbarians," such that the constant warfare caused them to look for a more peaceful home. They eventually invaded the British Isles, and the stories as a whole are titled "Invasion Myths." As a lover of myths and the kernels of truth they hide, I began to research this, along with many other odd stories.

Coincidentally, through a fluke of opportunity, I learned to play the Celtic Harp, a folk instrument that had its origins in ancient lands around the Mediterranean Sea: Syria, Egypt, Mycenae and lands even farther east. I learned there were no harps in ancient mainland European tradition, but that harps came across the Mediterranean to the British Isles, and then somehow all the way to Paraguay. The triangular instrument we recognize as a harp came very late to European lands, and eventually became the symphonic pedal harp. Those people who play that instrument are called "harpists," while those who play the original style of folk harp are called "harpers." Celtic tradition lauds these musicians as "bards," and harpers were absolutely important for keeping the histories of their people. With no system of writing, the oral histories were kept alive by these prominent people of the clan. Youths were trained early, in feats of memory and vocal ability. Every chieftain had a harper, and later, every nobleman and village retained a harper to record everything of importance for each clan or tribe.

Migrations of people can be traced by their cultural artifacts, their mode of dress, types of husbandry, their utensils, and their language. Nowadays, with our ability to research DNA, these migrations of peoples in very distant times can be mapped. While the dominant people of Ireland and Scotland came from the mainland of Europe, the specific tribe of those called "Scots-Irish" stand apart. These people wove tartan cloth, played the triangular instrument we know as a harp, and are further often identified as belonging to Haplogroup X. People in this insular group, both in customs and appearance, were predominantly Rh negative. Because of this genetic difference, the people were insular, that is, they did not often marry outside their tribe. Instead, their customs and language were different from the main population of Scotland or Ireland. Evidently, they came relatively late to the British Isles. Some historians record them as the "Dál Riada," who came to Scotland around 400AD. The language known as Gaelic transformed into modern day Scots Gàidhlig .

According to the DNA patterns, they must have been seafarers, because their genetic markers occur in populations of Berbers, Basques, Canary Islanders, Scots-Irish, and North American tribes such as the Ojibwa and Navajo. The markers also predominate the Ainu of Japan. These "bearded" Caucasian people are quite different than a typical Japanese person.

As I researched the history of the Celtic harp, I came upon the ancient oral manuscripts of Irish monks, written in Latin, who chronicled the stories called "Irish Invasion Myths." These stories tell of successive tribes invading the British Isles, those they conquered, and those who were victorious. One tribe was called the

"Tuatha Dé Danann," a tribe also referenced in ancient Egyptian records as the tribe of Dan or "the Danu." Egyptian sources describe them as part of the hegemony of "Sea Peoples," tribes of pirates that raided coastal cities. Some tribes were hired as mercenaries when Egyptians were fighting the Hittites, and were hired much later by the thirtieth pharaoh who actually had to invent the minting of gold coins, for they would not take payment in metaphoric loaves of bread. Only gold would suffice.

Additionally, in Scottish traditions there is a book called the "Scotichronicon," which also asserts this migration from the eastern Mediterranean, to a sojourn in Iberia, our modern countries of Portugal and Spain. Of course, people all over ancient Europe spoke a Celtic language form, for they called themselves "Galatians," "Gauls," "Galicians," or "Gaels." Their language was widespread throughout the Iberian Peninsula before the Romans invaded. The Romans rolled through Gaul in less than ten years, but fought in Iberia for over a hundred years until giving up the subjugation. The mixture of Latin with the ancient language can still be traced, as the surname "Gallegos" means Celt. Eventually the language mixed with Latin and became Spanish, Portuguese, or Gallagos. The more insular Basques seemed to keep their original tongue. The people in the British Isles don't refer to themselves as "Celts," but call themselves "Gaels."

Those oral histories, preserved by bards or harpers, were not given credence by later historians as anything more than folklore. The reason they were oral histories is because these ancient people had no written language, some say purposefully to avoid lies being preserved. In Spain, rare bronze tablets written with an ancient Phoenician alphabet told about a dispute over a proposed waterway. Beyond this, few examples of written language have ever been discovered. However, the translation revealed a Celtic language was spoken. Other than that, no rolls of papyrus or sheaves of parchment told their history. The Irish code language known as Ogham can be translated more easily into Basque than Gaelic, but that is for the linguistic archaeologists to dispute its origins.

The stories were eventually transcribed into Latin, again subject to much historical disbelief. However, the most amazing kernels of true history can be found in these legends. Battles and names of the victorious, subject to propaganda, must be viewed with more than a grain of salt. Amazingly, historically correct names also appear in these apocryphal stories, names that are actual historical people. Names of pharaohs, princesses, and a genealogy of royalty much like Biblical "begets" are listed. There are names of pharaohs that the Latin monks of 400AD could not have known!

Why? Because no one, not even the modern Egyptians themselves, could read the ancient hieroglyphs nor knew names of pharaohs, until the discovery and translation of the Rosetta Stone in 1822. Only after that could Egyptologists construct the dynasties of Egyptian rulers and learn the name of the thirtieth dynasty pharaohs, Nectanebo I and II. Egyptologists are now able to decipher prophecies, edicts, read inscriptions on monuments, and know that Nectanebo II actually lived circa 360 BCE. His regency can be accurately tied to a solar eclipse in 325 BCE, and the birth of Alexander the Great.

Nectanebo II was the last native-born Egyptian pharaoh, credited with ending the 30th dynasty. Ptolemaic rulers followed that dynasty and Egypt became ruled by Persians, Greeks, Romans, and eventually the British Empire. Though the tombs and mummies of this dynasty have never been found, Nectanebo II was an important leader during a turbulent time in Egypt. He was evidently victorious, for a while, in fighting the Persians, because his forces could accurately predict the Nile floods. Eventually Egypt fell, the Persians conquered Egypt, and they turned his beautiful granite sarcophagus into a bathtub by drilling a hole for a drain. Of course, they could not read the inscriptions. Nectanebo II was a prolific builder of temples, but his remains have never been found.

It is a surprise to find this pharaoh's name within the Irish legends. But there are no Egyptian records of the names of his wives or offspring; an earlier pharaoh seems to have been a cousin. Nor is it known how Nectanebus or Nectanebo I, who began the dynasty, came into power in the first place. He may have been important as a military leader. However, the mythical Irish stories also recount the escape of his daughter from Egypt to Ireland. Named Scota, or Scotach, perhaps as a nickname, we have no record of her historical name nor evidence that she was an actual historical person. According to legend, she was expected to marry her father, the pharaoh, as he had no sons. Instead, she and her husband Gamal Miledh, (from Miletus) fled to the shores of Spain and then Ireland. Thus, we have the legend that calls them "Milesians."

The novel *Scota's Harp* begins with this legend. Since this present novel is used as a sequel, it helps the reader to know the previous main plot, which follows here. With the use of an American Egyptologist, the novel exposes dozens of myths and legends that are revealed to have real, historical fact supporting them. Donald Cameron, the victim of unscrupulous artifact traders, is nearly murdered off the coast of Gibraltar. Before his near drowning, which results in hypoxia and memory loss, he mails an ancient papyrus to his sister Alison in America. She enlists the help of Professor Angus Morrison to help her find her lost brother. After finding him in hospital, the trio travel through Spain, Ireland, and Scotland before returning home. This journey allows the reader to discover connections between legends and reality, much like the trail of a treasure hunt. These myths and their meanings form the skeleton of the novel, where a different history is brought to light. The story weaves the following threads together, for a alternate history of the Stone of Scone, which is the Scottish Coronation Stone now in Edinburgh Castle:

- Milesians (Haplogroup X) invaded Ireland and named it after Scota's son Ir.

- Scotland is named for a tribe called "Scotti" after their queen, Scota.
- The Scottish coronation "Stone of Scone" brought by Scota, was inscribed to prove her royalty.
- Pharaoh Nectanebus II was believed to be the father of Alexander the Great in ancient times.
- Phillip of Macedonia divorced Olympia after her adultery with the "snake." (i.e. Nectanebus)
- Alexander the Great had horns at his temples, believed himself to be king of Egypt.
- Part of the Stone of Scone given to Ireland by Robert Bruce, is installed as the Blarney Stone.
- The stone Edward I stole was really a privy cover stone, not Scota's sacred stone.
- The stone stolen by students and returned to Scottish soil in 1950 was broken and repaired.
- The stone now residing in Edinburgh is not the authentic Stone of Scone.

This sequel to *Scota's Harp* begins with the agony of Donald Cameron suffering from post-traumatic-stress disorder or PTSD. He has no memory of his papyrus find in Spain, nor mailing it to America. His new wife, Valerie, knows nothing either, so unless Donald recovers his memory there will be no proof of the woman named Scota. It is doubtful that any of her true history will ever be found. Egyptologists completely discount the stories, and those researchers who dip into discrepancies in the accepted Egyptian chronology suffer derision and loss of acceptance in academic circles.

As I am only an "armchair researcher" and have no credentials as an archaeologist, this sequel to *Scota's Harp* is an effort to uncover other legends. My research reveals that the accepted chronology of Egyptian dynasties may be more than seven hundred years in error! By comparing historical documents of Persians, Ethiopians, Hittites, and Hebrew rulers, researchers have constructed an acceptable history of these cultures, but one that may be rife with propaganda about victorious wars and lengths of reigns that may or may not be accurate. Radiocarbon dates are not specific enough to give accurate dates. We must rely on astronomical dates that coincide with dates of a solar eclipse or Sirius rising, accurately measured by cross-referenced observations by Persians and Egyptians This is how we know Alexander the Great was born in 325 BCE.

Today, many researchers of ancient history believe there really was a "Battle of Troy," and that this once great city lay on the coast of Anatolia. Other people believe Homer's stories of the Iliad and *Odyssey* are just a collection of fables and fantasy, an effort to explain the foibles of the Olympian deities. In this sequel, I intend to show that nine tribes of "Sea Peoples" did attack Egypt, as depicted at the temple of Medinet Habu; the illustrations depict Ramses III's victory over these pillagers.

Archaeologists have proven that a famous city once thrived on the Anatolian coast. It may have been called Wilusa in ancient times. However, if Homer's opus has any historical fact, there is no way for me to believe that the great seafarer, Ulysses, would be lost for ten or twenty years in the Mediterranean, or the "Tyrrhenian Sea" as they called it. He would have known his way home to nearby Ithaka. Perhaps that is not where he was going.

A close reading of the *Odyssey* gives many landmarks, enough to describe a voyage but one not in the Mediterranean at all. Instead come with me and take a trip all the way north to Scotland's Outer and Inner Hebrides. There you would see the legendary whirlpool of Corryvreckan, off the coast of the Isles of Jura and Mull.

I have added a Glossary, words with which you may not be familiar. Perhaps peruse this before you start on the journey I've put before you. I hope you enjoy the read.

-- Michele Buchanan

1

Cold bedsheets were slick with sweat when Donald Cameron woke. Instantly the realization hit that Val must have retreated to the couch, safe from his thrashing feet. Waves of sadness crashed over him. His mouth even tasted like salty sand from the delusion of his nightmare. Uncontrollable shivering belied the fact that an exceedingly hot, stifling July of summer heat had taken over the Illinois prairie. It was little relief that this time he could at least remember his name and know he really was safe at home. With other nightmares long ago, he had not been so privileged. Although the night terrors were getting less frequent, and usually happened only in July, he wondered if he would ever conquer the amnesia and hypoxia he suffered in Gibraltar so long ago. Try as he might, the happiness and peace he should have as a young father, being happily married, and the achievement of college professorship for which he had worked so hard, seemed denied him.

Shaking off the rushing sounds of waves in his head, Donnie controlled his breathing and forced his spasming muscles to relax. He smelled the humid hot air wafting through the open window and took a deep, long breath. He hesitated before coming upright as his jellied legs remained convinced that he was drowning in ocean waves. Like some ancient pagan Pict thrown to the depths as a sacrifice, somehow he had survived. But no one would pull him to safety. He had to save himself. He opened his eyes to watch the crack of dawn enter the room, trying to pierce the thick air as if it too were viscous water.

In summer, most folks in Illinois slept on back porches, screened in from buzzing insects, although some comfort came that the heat brought out the fireflies. At least fireflies could light up a mason jar and provide wonder for the kids. The drone of cicadas would be gone with the end of July, but it was early in the month. And Donald Cameron had most of the vacation month ahead of him.

Valerie slept within hearing distance of the bedroom, in case Donnie thrashed hard enough to throw himself onto the floor. Wildly kicking legs, choking coughs, and beating the mattress into a pulp made sleeping beside him dangerous in July. Various medications had been tried, but so far nothing could unlock the cause of this PTSD that raged like a shark-feeding frenzy. Val had sought out specialists, even those knowledgeable in hypnotic regression, but the trauma seemed to be like a hopelessly blocked sewage pipe that would never empty. Did his brain contain the stink of some heinous crime or misbehavior causing a lost love? That nightmarish circular loop of memory coursed with the force of a demon, eating his sense of security and threatening his marriage. He was helpless as a beached fish when he gave himself up to sleep in July.

Their children, Andrew, now seven, and Sadie, just five, never noticed this behavior of their parents sleeping separately, as the kids slept soundly in their bedroom after story time each night. Donnie had moved from all the primarily children's books by Dr. Seuss and other usual titles, and now read more advanced books. Donnie was a world class storyteller, and with the addition of Andrew Lang's version of Homer's *Ulysses*, *Arabian Nights* and *Aesop's Fables* he enthralled his children as much as his father, Mungo Cameron, had mesmerized him. But both sets of grandparents had long ago passed. Perhaps Donnie's stories were told with the private hope that he might infuse his own dreams with a pleasant fairy tale, one that ended with justice and satisfaction. He preferred Disney versions over any of those by the Brothers Grimm, and his children looked forward to story time at day's end. Donnie repeated certain favorite stories so often that Sadie had learned to read by hearing them. Alternating stories between what Andrew considered "baby books" and more mature stories such as the *Bobbsey Twins* or *Hardy Boys* kept both children interested. Sadie was excited to be entering school in the Fall. At least her behavior didn't predict any of the problems they'd had with Andrew when he entered school.

One teacher even maintained that Andrew was hyperactive and needed medication. Val managed to get him switched to another classroom that year, and Andrew managed better behavior. Did teachers just hate redheads? That might have been part of it. Both parents had had their share of teasing in school, and not just from classmates. Still it was a common theme, a higher activity level and a curiosity that needed consistent interesting challenges. Neither kid would sit still for anything boring.

Only the lack of commotion in their room meant that the kids were still in bed. Donnie got up, threw on his white Jacobite shirt with the puffy sleeves and cross-laced neckline. Over this, he belted on his Cameron tartan kilt, latched buckles at the waist and thigh. He tiptoed barefooted into the kitchen. His cabled knee socks could wait with the other pieces of his clan costume. He turned on the coffeemaker, then checked the fridge for eggs. Lacy curtains spilled sunlit patterns on the tile floor as the rosy fingers of dawn brought color to the room. "Anyone for pancakes today?" he called. He knew the kids would be awake momentarily, because of the promised excitement of the day ahead.

"Make mine look like a duck!" ordered Sadie as she bounded into the kitchen, teddy bear in one hand, her Cameron sash in the other. She had already pulled on her tartan skirt. Sarah, or "Sadie" as they called her, was as freckled and red-haired as any Strawberry Shortcake doll, but twice as cute. Actually, she looked just like her mother's childhood photos, as Val had the same red hair and freckles. Her Irish heritage came through just as strong as Donnie's

Scottish genes, so the kids had no chance of avoiding being "gingers." What was it about redheads that made them seem so full of life? Behaviorists had identified a few factors that seemed to predominate, one being risk-takers or hyperactivity. No one knows if this propensity is genetic or learned because of how others treated them, but both Donnie and Valerie knew they had a couple of very active kids on their hands.

Moments later, Andrew came tearing in. This kid ran everywhere, all the time. He fumbled with his kilt buckles and the sporran was nearly flying loose. Val came in, smothered Sadie with a hug and kisses, saying "Good morning, Sunshine," then did the same to her husband. Donnie looked at her, his eyes asking, *Everything ok?* She answered silently with a loving smile and got out the plates.

Val set the table, honoring the agreed rule that those who cook don't do the set-up or clean-up, and Donnie was cooking today. Andrew's chores were to make his bed and help take out the trash. Sadie's responsibility was to make sure mommy's keys were hung on the key hook whenever they returned from an outing. Although both parents were trained archeologists, Donnie was the "chief finder" of lost things. In fact, that was how he'd met Val in the first place, by finding Roman coins at a Celtic site in Spain. Coins are easily transported, and keys get lost just as often. The family relied on that key hook to save time whenever they were going out because Val had a habit of tossing the keys down, wherever, when she entered the house with groceries in hand. And today, they were going near Springfield, about an hour away, to attend the Illinois Highland Games.

The family would all be dressed in Cameron tartan to march with clan members in the opening ceremonies. In all his gear, Donnie looked the part of an ancient Highlander with his kilt, Jacobite shirt, and red hair poking out from under his war bonnet. His checkered hat, adorned with a white cockade and clan crest brooch, made him look like some tall Highland chieftain. The cut of his chin, broad face and blue-green eyes announced his Scottish ancestry.

Andrew, tall for his age, also had auburn hair and freckles like some modern-day Huck Finn. He was boisterous and liked to clown around, sometimes teasing his little sister or hurting her feelings. Today he wore a regular child-sized kilt and child's sporran, but no *sgian dubh* yet. Besides, in the heat of summer, wearing sandals without knee-socks, there would be nowhere to secure the small knife traditionally tucked in the sock at the right calf.

Valerie wore a floor length tartan skirt, white peasant blouse and a long tartan sash affixed at the shoulder with a clan brooch. The only thing out of place was her shoulder purse, in which she carried all the various modern needs of wallet and credit cards. Also, the netted reticule that hung off the belt at her waist only had room for a small flask of Scottish whisky.

The family hadn't found any authentic Cameron tartan articles for Sadie to wear yet, except for a short sash. Val hoped they'd find a skirt or fabric at the festival today as there would be many vendors of Scottish items. Wool tartan fabric was usually too expensive, but sometimes at these festivals authentic tartan weaves could be found in cotton or acrylics, which would be more easily laundered than that coming directly from some Scottish mill. Sadie came bounding into the kitchen with her sash flying like a kite. Val fixed her sash at the shoulder with a little thistle pin. When she was all set, Sadie began dancing and twirling around the kitchen, arms up in a Highland fling imitation.

"She doesn't need dance lessons," complimented Andrew. This was unusual, as Andrew often teased his little sister. He might have preferred a brother, but Sadie was a girl, so he had to share a bedroom with her and hundreds of stuffed animals. At least his comment caused Val to smile and she laughed as she held her daughter's hands and twirled her around. Sadie held her fingers like deer antlers, and smiled proudly as if she really knew what she was doing.

All they needed was music. Andrew started to pretend playing bag-pipes, just tooting as he followed Sadie around the kitchen. Then Donnie called everyone to the table for pancakes. The excitement seemed to overflow like the syrup and butter swirling on the plates. Donnie poured coffee for himself and Val, and milk for the kids. The kitchen smelled like pancakes in the hot morning air.

Because the Celtic festival in Springfield was a two-day af-fair, many families brought their campers to stay overnight. For Don and Val however, even motel lodging nearby seemed too costly, so they would stay but one day. Even so, a single day would give them enough time and fun to see all the events. Usually there would be a herd of sheep and a flock of ducks for the working dogs to put on a show. At the "working dog" demonstration, the dog owner would direct his dog either with hand signals or short whistles, and he would deftly direct the sheep back into their pen.

Other dogs would race after a lure on a wire. Of all the dog breeds Donnie expected to see, he thought the Scottish Deerhounds were the best. Their calm nature belied the amazing speed they could muster while chasing prey. Still, the Shelties and Border Collies might be the most intelligent. When Donnie and Val were on the Isle of Lewis, in the Outer Hebrides archipelago of Scotland, the people told them how their dog would be in charge of bringing sheep to market all the way to the mainland. They'd tell the dog which person to deliver the sheep to, have them board the ferry, and bring them safely to market. Friends along the way would see that the dog got fed if it was an overnight trip, then the dog would go back to the ferry alone, and get home. Those dogs were invaluable. And of course, there would be Scottish Terriers, Corgis, and Irish Water Spaniels to admire. Usually there would be a dog and owner parade, with each dog wearing a tartan flash on their collar. Donnie knew his kids desperately wanted a dog. Valerie wanted them to have one each.

There would be other animals, too. Huge horses called Clydesdales showed off long-haired manes, tails, and feet. Horse lovers might also see Percherons, Morgans, or Shires, maybe a huge draft horse, as well as Shetland ponies. It was a common practice to parade the horses around the grounds, visit Clan booths, and let children experience the size of a champion horse. Last year the Percheron displayed at the games had a height of nineteen hands, which is well over six feet at the shoulders. Their massive size and strength are amazing to behold.

Many Festival goers came to hear the bagpipe contest and watch the Scottish and Irish dance competitions, while the most-attended attraction was the caber toss. Men built like tree trunks attempted to throw the wooden pole up into the air and complete an end-over-end somersault in order to count. Other events included the stone throw, a chained stone spun around like a discus and then thrown. And there were "rocks for weight" that simply required a strong man to lift it and carry for distance. These events were called "heavy athletics" for good reason.

Donnie smiled from ear to ear, enjoying this early morning scene of his family as if it were a painting by Norman Rockwell. His pride teetered as if on the edge of a precipice he was so happy. Underneath it all, he knew something loomed in the back of his mind, something he repressed in the bright light of day.

With breakfast soon over and dishes put in the dishwasher, they loaded into the Rover. Val plied sunscreen on everyone's noses, and put straw hats on Sadie and herself. After they were all safely buckled in, Donnie looked at Val. *Everything ok?* his eyes asked. Her smiling face assured Donnie that they were "one for all, and all for one."

True to her marriage vows, Val supported Donnie in every way possible. They had met so casually, at Neolithic ruins in Spain, that it was like "kismet" or a match made in heaven. When they would tell other couples how they came to be married, the story was usually met with disbelief, because "love at first sight" is such a fairytale. Even as a young girl, Val was confident and satisfied with living alone, and exploring the world on her own. As a risk taker, she was confident, and often joked that she made choices on the spot. But given the opportunity to travel to Ireland with Donnie, his sister Alison, and Dr. Morrison, she felt a camaraderie that she couldn't pass up. It became the family she'd always wanted, and she valued every minute. Donnie's nightmares had no power over her love and admiration for the man she considered a great catch.

"Are you going to enter the events?" asked Andrew as their car travelled over the highway.

"No, those men who compete travel all over the country, earning points for national rankings. I'm out of their league. And it can be dangerous if you haven't practiced how to do things, like swing a rock on a chain around your shoulders. The cabers can pass for telephone poles, each graded by weight and length. That's not for me. I'm strong, but not that strong. Imagine me just trying to pick the thing up? Just 'cause I can toss you around like a sack of potatoes, that wouldn't cut it."

Andrew nodded with understanding. He'd seen the competition before.

Then Sadie piped up, saying, "But Mommy could do the one where the ladies throw the straw over the pole. She's good at tossing me up in the air." Everyone laughed at the thought.

On the drive, Donnie played a Scottish music CD, turned up the volume and had everyone singing "Flower of Scotland," "Bonnie Dundee" and the "March of the Cameron Men." Andrew drummed on the back of the front seat pretending he had a *bodhrán*. Sadie clapped her hands matching her brother's beat. Donnie and Val sang in harmony, proud of their children and their obvious excitement and knowledge of Scottish heritage. Over the next rise they saw the festival tents, banners flying, and could hear the sound of bagpipes skirling. Even before they found a parking spot, they could smell delicious food in the air.

After parking, the family got their entrance wristbands and set off to enjoy the festival. The program had a map of the layout: kid's area, clan booths, food trucks, and dance tents circled around a central covered stage for musicians. The athletic events and bagpiping competitions were further out on huge fields. The dance competitors had separate canopies over wooden dance floors, and chairs for the spectators. As the Cameron family walked into the festival area, they could see that each food truck already had a line of hungry people. You could sample haggis or even Black or White dumplings, and all sorts of wonderful pastries. Scottish shortbread would be for sale after the judges had chosen their favorites, and most of the food trucks had varieties of scones and praties.

The family walked first to the kid's area where both children got involved in Nerf archery and Nerf swordplay. Some older children were putting on a display of jousting with wooden shields and tin pie-plate armor. Donnie and Val moved out of earshot.

"Sorry to frighten you outa bed last night," said Donnie. "I don't even remember what was happening in the dream. . . as usual."

"It's ok," said Val quietly. "But you're supposed to keep notes on the note pad by the bed. Doctor's orders. Remember anything at all?"

"Nope, just fear. Just thinking about tide waters, trying to orient and go with the flow."

"I think it's time we try again to open this can of worms. Maybe your sister has information she could tell us. Could you ask her sometime? Again? Since hypnotism didn't work, and sleeping pills only make it worse, maybe it's time to ask her again. All she told me is that somehow you swam from off the coast to Gibraltar, and that she found you unconscious in the hospital. It's not fair to not know what happened to you. Seven years of this is enough. I don't mean to nag. It just gets to me to see you suffering. And I don't like sleeping alone."

Donnie nodded, watching their kids having fun in the hot sunshine. "I guess I thought somehow I'd get better on my own. You know I nearly drowned. But there must be some other secret locked up, must be serious. I trust you to talk to her, instead of me, just in case it's stuff that could be worse. Else why hasn't she offered that info already?"

"Ok, I'll call her when we get home. She doesn't know how much you are still suffering since we only see her if we go to California. The kids would really enjoy a trip to Disneyland. Can you get some vacation time before the Fall semester? It would be a great surprise for us all to have one last trip before you are lost in research."

"My chairperson is still struggling with that weird find we exposed when you were pregnant with Andrew. That publication seems stuck in his craw. Maybe the publish or perish pressure is part of my problem. That alone is enough anxiety for ten men. It'd be good to get away for a week or so. You're right." Donnie and Val embraced. She was clear-eyed, smiled, and always offered support. She hated putting any more pressure on him; that was the last thing he needed. Val knew in her heart just how far to push. Not that Donnie was still the fragile lost puppy she'd met in Spain, but she understood his current quagmire in the department.

"Why don't you take Andrew to see the athletics, and I'll take Sadie through some of the other attractions. We'll meet up just before noon for the parade?" said Val.

"Ok, good plan. I know he wants to check out the Boy Scouts booth, and the caber toss will be happening first thing. See you later." Donnie went off to get Andrew away from nerf jousting.

Val took Sadie by the hand, and they strolled past booth after colorful booth. Every clan had their flags waving, maps of their clan territories, and clan histories and literature. The Buchanan clan was showing off their many varieties of Scotch whisky, all varieties of single malt brewed by their clan. One bottle labeled "Black and White" sported the drawing of two Scottie dogs on the label. The clan also flew a flag with a black rampant lion, evidently because at one time the Buchanan chief was next in line to the throne.

As they rounded the end of "Clan Row" they came upon a group of ladies seated around a long table. There were eight chairs, but two were vacant, and one woman motioned for Val and Sadie to take seats.

"We are demonstrating 'waulking the cloth' and we need all the seats filled. Please join us for a song or two?"

Val happily took a seat with Sadie next to her, and saw before them an upright plastic stand with words to follow along for singing. A length of blue and green tartan plaid was looped around the table, in front of each person to handle.

"I am the caller on this song," said Maura MacNeill. "We sing most of our songs in *Gàidhlig*, the Scottish form of Gaelic. "But our next song will be in English. You'll catch on right away. All you have to do is match this sequence." She demonstrated by grabbing the fabric, slamming it down, then forward, then back, and passing it to the left. "By passing the looped wool to the singer on your left the wool travels around the table while we sing."

She then explained in a loud voice to everyone passing by, as their booth had drawn quite a crowd of onlookers: "The women of the Isles do a lot of weaving all winter, for the nights are very long so far north. When they've woven a good length of wool, it needs more treatment before it can be cut or sewn into a garment, because the weave is still loose. It would just ravel out if it wasn't 'fulled' to just the right thickness. When summer comes the ladies bring all their wool to the village center, sort of like a quilting bee. The loop of wool is put on a long table that has a groove down the center, and that's where the mordant is poured, to dip the wool into. Traditionally the mordant is uric acid, pretty stinky. 'Stale urine'" she whispered humorously. "You don't want to sit at the low end of the table since the liquid flows downhill."

"After the wool is pounded on the table, and repeatedly dipped into the mordant, the wool will be colorfast and waterproof. The lady whose wool is being worked on will be the singer, or caller, and she would decide when her piece is finished. In the Hebrides, women would do this summer work for fourteen or more hours a day, and of course the songs had a lot of gossip about whatever happened in the preceding winter. Lots of love stories, or who married who."

After a few practice movements with the wool, and seeing that Sadie had the movements ok, the leader of the group started off a song in English.

> White the sheep that gave the wool
> Green the pastures where they fed
> Blue and scarlet side by side,
> Bless the warp and bless the thread.
>
> Bless the man who wears this cloth
> May he wounded never be
> From the bitter cold and frost
> May this cloth protection be.

There were three more verses to the song, and Sadie was giggling and having so much fun. The leader of the group brought in some more bystanders to sing the next song, but Sadie kept her seat.

"You're wearing Cameron tartan?" the leader noticed as she and Val stepped away a space. "I've been doing this demo for many years and learned to identify the tartans. My MacNeil is used in the demo you practiced on. It's dry of course, but the navy-blue alternates with a thin red and a thin white line, easy to identify. Your Cameron is lovely."

"Thanks" said Val, "my husband and I travelled to the Isle of Lewis eight years ago before we were married. He's an archaeologist, and now teaches at Bloomington. We've come up for the day with our two kids. Sadie is really enjoying your singing. It is a wonderful tradition you are teaching."

"Well, the MacNeill clan was historically a bunch of pirates. Their homestead is on Barra, in Kisimul Castle. You might have seen it if you passed by Mull. The castle is on a huge rock in the water, cut off from the mainland. But it has a freshwater spring that supplies the castle with water. The sailors were caught and tried as pirates by James VI, and now it's a tourist attraction. One of our songs is 'Kisimul's Galley,' that tells about sailors coming home.

"What kind of boats did they have? I know the sea around that area can't allow big ships."

"According to the song, the galley just had a rudder, no mast or 'ring,' and it was manned by rowing. They steered by rowing. Pretty amazing, actually. There are ancient archaeological remains that show habitation on the Isles that dates to over six thousand years back."

"That would have been Neolithic Era" said Val. "I'm an archaeologist too."

"I think it's important for the youngsters to know how their wool gets to market," said Maura. "We try to keep the traditions going."

Val thanked Maura for all that she learned, then went to get Sadie. She was singing "Shane Oli" repeatedly, which evidently meant "sing out." Then mother and daughter went speedily over to the main staging area to find Donnie and Andrew. There would be a clan parade at the opening ceremonies, and various societies would be represented. All would be led by a color guard carrying the national flag. Pipe bands would be arranged en masse, and would lead all the people in a parade to the front speakers.

Traditionally, the opening ceremonies start at noon, and Val and Sadie found the boys already in line. Their Cameron family joined in with about fifteen other people dressed in Cameron tartan, and one man held a pole that held the Cameron crest banner. Since it was alphabetical order, they assembled just ahead of the Campbells, whose tartan was mostly green. There were over twenty clans in attendance; banners and clan crests flew in the breeze. It was a sunny day, not meant for Scottish wool, and the bagpipers were obviously hot in their black jackets. Everyone was anxious to start marching and to hear the sound of "Scotland the Brave" filling the air.

Crowds of people lined the parade route, cheering to the stirring sound of massed pipe bands. After the short march to the front staging area, the pipe major signaled a halt, and the bagpipers were at ease. The pipers began tuning up their reeds as the clans' members got organized. Then a lady sang the National Anthem and the crowd cheered.

There was a hush as various speakers were introduced, the "honored guest" and other dignitaries gave opening remarks. After all the speeches Donnie quizzed Andrew.

"Remember what some of the clan names mean? Remember Cameron?"

"Well, a 'cam' is like a gear, or a crooked thing," replied Andrew, "and 'ron' means face. At least ours doesn't mean 'crooked mouth' or 'liar' like the Campbells."

"What about those Buchanan's in front of us?" asked Donnie.

"Did they have canons?" asked Andrew.

"No, their name means the support or base of the 'canon' which is a set of laws for a church."

"That's cool," said Andrew. "I bet none of my friends know that names have old meanings. Cameron's are the greatest!" As if repeating the exclamation, they heard the snare drums beat everyone to attention. The pipe major raised his baton, and the pipe bands led them all in a march to the front of the gathering crowds.

The announcer called out each clan name when their group came to the front of the podium. Each clan would acknowledge the honor by signaling with their clan banner or flag. Donnie's skin prickled with pride to see his little family carry on such long-held traditions. Perhaps it was time for another trip "over the pond." At least now Sadie would be old enough to remember the trip.

After the parade dispersed, Val suggested they get something to eat.

"How about some Scotch eggs or a fried pickle?" jested Donnie.

Val laughed. Most of the food trucks offered fried things to eat, even fried ice cream. She settled on hot dogs for the kids and meat pies for Donnie and herself. She bought three bottles of Irn Bru, the Scottish soft drink so overrated by Scots. Val also asked for two paper cups with ice so she could give each of the kids a taste. Although it would quench their thirst, it was full of sugar, and Val didn't want Andrew to have more than his usual energy. After a few sips of the orange soda, Sadie decided it had no taste and poured hers out. Andrew slugged it down, then both kids re-filled their cups with water. They found a vacant table to sit at in limited shade, cleaned up their trash, and headed off to see more of the festival. The girls wanted to watch the fiddle competition, Irish step dancing, and Scottish dancers competing to the tune of a piper. Donnie and Andrew intended to watch more of the athletics. At the end of "clan row," there were booths for various societies: Irish Americans, Scottish Americans, and even Scandinavians. Andrew ran off ahead, rounded a corner, and then yelled back, "Hey Dad, they got a Trojan Horse!"

Sure enough, in front of them stood a ten-foot statue of a horse on a flatbed trailer. The bright neon-pink horse, decorated with flowers, blue bridle and ribbons, had flowers laced into its plati-num blonde tail. Donnie's heart skipped a beat while he stood there, awestruck.

"Dala horse," explained the exhibitor. "Scandinavian fathers carved small wooden Dala horses for their children to play with while they were away doing Viking things. It's a traditional toy for children." Donnie stood there with a quizzical look as the vendor directed him to his bin of little carved horses. Donnie bought two horses, much to Sadie's delight, though it was doubtful Andrew would ever play with the little carving. Val's shopping bag was now bulging with a new Scottish flag, some lapel pins, and a green wool tam for Sadie. She'd bought some sandwiches and drinks for the ride home, but the bagpipe music would hang in their memories until Burns' Night came around in January. Their excursion had been a perfect day, except that Donnie was lost in thought. He couldn't get over seeing that huge horse.

2

On the ride home, both kids had fallen sound asleep in the car. Val got Andrew to wake up and get moving, while Donnie just carried Sadie into the house. Val helped the children into their pajamas and got them to brush their teeth then she packed their wool tartan garments into the cedar chest to protect them from moths. Shirts went into the laundry basket, catchup stains and all. Sadie hid the little Dala horses between some stuffed bears and hopped into bed. Andrew would never miss them; he was too interested in remote-control race cars. Besides, he was always hiding her favorite bear or bunny.

"Who wants a story? Or are you too tired?" Donnie asked. Sadie was already sound asleep as Donnie carried her to her bed, and Andrew's eyelids were heavy. They'd had an action-packed long day, and Andrew had run all around the fields and had used up his usual energy. Val came to check on them too, closed their bedroom door, then got two cold beers for a quiet evening on the back porch. Donnie met with Val outside, but he had a far-away look in his eyes, thinking about what he'd seen today. The Dala horse was distracting, not surprising since Donnie's head was mostly in Egypt, but it reminded him of something in one of the Lang fables. Somehow that huge horse just didn't fit, though the Scandinavians always had a booth at the games.

There was a cooling breeze on the back porch as they settled into the porch swing, but it was still hot, even at night.

"That Dala horse is a new one on me," said Donnie. "I never think of horses with Vikings, or any of the northern cultures, do you?"

"No, you're right. I don't think the Dala horse ever came up in my basic studies, nothing in Celtiberian stuff either. But they did use chariots. Maybe do some research on that one. I know there is some graphic metalwork using horse symbolism, but it's very minor. Not a central theme like the man stressed at the booth today. And I thought it would be an odd thing for a father to give his child to remember him by. Seems like something more obviously Scandinavian would be more like it, like a wooden goat."

Donnie chuckled. "Yeah, our friend in Sweden sent us that straw goat for Christmas one year, like it was something special they do. Revere a goat? It's funny that Andrew immediately thought of the Trojan Horse story. You know I've read Lang's rewrite of Homer's work to him. It's easier for kids to relate to the *Odyssey* without all the flowery words. But I just can't get that big statue out of my mind." He sipped thoughtfully at the bottle, the beer was good and cold on such a hot evening. They sat quietly, looking at stars, mulling over their experiences of what would be a memorable day. The Milky Way coursed like a river in the sky, and Donnie thought about the rising of stars that might have steered Vikings on a long journey. He finished his beer, looked over at Val, and thought how lucky he was to have her. Before words came out of his mouth, Val stood up.

"It's been a long day, really fun, but I'm pooped," said Val. "Wish there was a stronger breeze now though. It's too hot for me. You gonna watch the fireflies awhile? I'm off to bed." She hugged and kissed her husband, said "Love you," and took the empty bottles to the kitchen. Donnie sat alone, lost in thought. He had hoped for a more romantic message from Val, but taking two kids to the festival had been exhausting.

Donnie mused about the "Viking" find they had uncovered years ago in the middle of that nondescript Illinois prairie. It had been thoroughly researched and documented. Dated to about the first century A.D., the burial had artifacts for a Norse chieftain's grave but no mortal remains. It did have sufficient metal weapons, shields, and leather trappings to have been Scandinavian in nature. Some of the leather items had knotwork designs, and one decrepit dagger was inscribed with Norse runes. Donnie and Val had proven, at least in academic circles, that the Norsemen had "discovered" the American continent long before Columbus. They knew of other odd finds even farther west, but their find proved that Norsemen had explored much further than Nova Scotia or America's east coast. Val's expertise had been with the "Mound Builder" culture which had its share of controversies. It seemed that whichever culture they investigated, anomalous artifacts would surface. Whenever this happens, the finder might be accused of "salting" the dig, or excavating in a sloppy way. Such academic stodginess seemed cast in concrete. It was always a battle against the establishment when it came to beliefs in the face of new theories. And anomalous artifacts always shook up the established academia.

So, their find in Illinois was unique, out of place, and controversial. Writing it up had been an uphill battle, but the site was worth some headlines in academia. If explorers could cross the oceans and somehow get lost in Illinois, there was no reason in Donnie's mind to discount the ability of Celts or Norsemen to invade as far as the Mediterranean. Seas and major rivers were their swift highways. Brave seamen, who trusted their strength of arm with oars, could go wherever water would take them. Those ancient boats, of hardened leather and ribbed with wood, could be portaged if needed. An ancient galley of forty men could conquer villages, reap the spoils, and revel in their life on the sea.

Donnie knew all the finer points separating the Celts from the Norsemen, but knew their cultures were entwined. DNA research showed they intermarried, and as sailors of the sea, they forged alliances as raiders far and wide. Several settlements in Scotland revealed the traditional rectangular houses of the Norsemen right alongside the typical round dwellings of the Celts. Even the knotwork people nowadays consider "Celtic" is really more Scandinavian in mythos, just different gods were worshipped. As Donnie thought more about this subject, he fell asleep on the chaise lounge on the back porch, and drifted into dreamland thinking about the Battle of Troy. And a Trojan Horse painted neon pink.

Somewhere around 3:00 am. Donnie entered his usual nightmare. He was floating in cold water, trying to keep from drowning, choking on beer that came up from his stomach. For once, however, he visualized images and this time he controlled the dream as if it were a movie. It was the Trojan War, and he was not in Gibraltar. Greeks had just deposited a huge wooden horse outside the gates of Troy. Other warriors were charging through the low surf, and Donnie was among them. They were intent on storming the city now that the city gates had been opened. Donnie knew the ancient story well, so his dream played out a scene of silent Greeks dropping out of a wooden horse that had been brought into the city walls. There were other images in this dream. A man he imagined must be Odysseus, wept with shame, as if this ruse was not an honorable way to win the advantage.

Oddly, in Donnie's dream, the Greeks looked wrong. His imagination dressed them in wool kilts, and horned helmets, not like the typical Greek skullcap. He was with them, dressed in his Cameron kilt, and he had a huge claymore sword to wield. Nor were the others armed as Greeks. Instead their weapons were inscribed with Celtic knotwork and the men wore gold torques around their necks which ended in dragon's heads. Their beards were stiffened with salt spray like wild men of an ancient forest. The dream was so clear to Donnie, that these invaders were not Greeks, but pirates from somewhere far away north. Another word stuck in his mind, "Danite."

Instead of thrashing and falling off the porch chair, Donnie woke with a start. He was sweaty, but calm. Relieved and wide awake, he went to the bedroom, found the writing pad, and jotted down a few words to jog his memory in the morning. Then he crawled into bed next to Val, and slept soundly. His dream had evolved into an odd theory, one that he could pursue, that would take his sleeping hours down a different path. He was almost in control of the dream. He had a new plan, one that didn't involve calling Ali. Maybe it was just a distraction, but it seemed to Donnie that he would be able to interpose a different narrative while dreaming. After all, daytime work, intensely compelling as was this subject, might just be the ticket out of his PTSD.

3

Early that morning, Val woke, pleased that it was Sunday, with no urgency to get up at any special time. She smiled when she realized her husband was sleeping soundly next to her. She heard his soft breathing. He was calm and not crouched in the usual fetal position. Through the sultry night the sheets wound up on the floor, her nightgown massed itself around her thighs, but a cool breeze wafted through the window. She reached out tentatively, put her hand on his shoulder and whispered, "So nice to have you here."

Donnie woke, opened his eyes and kissed her. "Something weird happened last night," he whispered, "I mean good, not scary."

"You mean, no nightmare?"

"Somehow I was able to distract myself into thinking about the Battle of Troy" said Donnie. "I imagined that the Trojan horse was pink and decked with flowers like the horse we saw at the festival. It was really funny for a while. I guess dreams can replay some daytime events?"

"I've been reading some dream research," said Val. "There is something called 'lucid dreaming,' where people can control their dreams, at least partly. One lady described it as 'visiting her library,' taking out a dream volume, and picking it up where she left off. Maybe you can learn to do it?"

"Wow! Never heard of that. I'll look into it. Train myself? If I can do that, maybe I can even do research while dreaming. I sure am tired of those nightmares. What do you think about Celts being at the Battle of Troy? I know they traveled all around the North

Sea... and there's the 'Brendan Voyage' where some monk went to Greenland. Ever hear of it?"

Val responded, "No, and that's hard to believe. The voyage must have been terrifying."

"Well, the ancient mariners knew what they were doing. I think they could have gone anywhere, even great distances. You know, just this year three Scottish brothers set the record for rowing across the Atlantic. They left the Canary Islands and got to Antigua thirty-five days later. The MacLean clan honored them with a trophy, I guess. Sailing might have been so common that people traded goods from all sorts of places."

"I can't imagine rowing across the Atlantic! Crazy Scots! But aren't there some big boats and sailors depicted in Egyptian reliefs that looked like foreigners? It might even be the same time period?"

"You're right about those inscriptions. Maybe my dream was related to new research I'm doing with Dr. Morrison. Could be my subconscious trying to get me to research Celts or Gaels instead of Vikings."

"I'll make breakfast. Let the kids sleep longer while you get on the computer. How about scrambled eggs?"

"Sounds great! Love ya," Donnie gave his wife a loving embrace, threw on some clothes and went into his office area. He could set the table later, but right now he wanted to look at research that might connect seafarers with Troy. He felt like a new man. *Guess that's what a good night's sleep does for these bones*, thought Donnie. Val went to the kitchen. The kids would sleep at least another hour. There was no hurry for breakfast anyway, they weren't going anywhere today.

In a side room that served as his home office, Donnie looked through stacks of print-outs about a temple named Medinet Habu. His method of organization was easy for him, though to anyone else his office looked like a rat's nest. One main stack of papers was devoted to 18th dynasty pharaohs, while another stack concerned

23

only 26th dynasty leaders. Another pile amassed information about the last native Egyptian dynasty, the 30th. Over in the corner were the documents about their finds in Illinois, their "Viking" hoard, and next to that were reports of other North American anomalies. That stack was getting larger, and had captured Donnie's interest for the last seven years. There were plenty of axe head finds that weren't native American, all over the continent. Of course, no one could date stone without other carbon-based items, so they were just oddities, left by some travelers long ago. Val also wanted to investigate American Indian sites because they were especially prone to pot hunters and unscrupulous adventurers. She knew that the unexplored and undocumented sites were in danger of destruction, and felt that more interest should be paid to them. Little funding went that way of course, maybe because no one could expect to find a pharaoh's gold death mask. Research into Egyptian chronology, though immensely interesting to Donnie, would only lead to more brick walls. Val knew her goal was to support Donnie, and she loved being his sidekick, and she knew their lives would never be boring.

Donnie warmed up his computer and looked at sites that talked about Troy. He had not really thought about that period of history until recently, so diverted was he with North America. Controversy surrounded dating the major battle of Troy, if indeed it had actually happened at all. Many researchers believed the battle and story were just made up, but after Hisarlik and those areas of eastern Turkey were opened to archaeologists, many layers of an ancient city were found. In fact, there were ten layers of habitation, and several layers, numbered VI and VII were thought to evidence a huge conflagration of a city. This was identified as actual Troy. Controversies abounded with dating the finds, as usual in archaeology, but the consensus was that a huge battle had occurred in 1186 BCE. This would have been Late Bronze Age, and Donnie knew this would have been a period of high civilization in Egypt. He knew the accepted chronology of pharaohs by heart. But historians such as Strabo, Plutarch and Thucydides thought the battle of Troy had no validity. They talked about battles in the North Atlantic. It had always bothered Donnie that the stories of the *Iliad* and *Odyssey* had two names for the hero. The Greeks called him Odysseus while the more recent Romans and English speakers called him Ulysses. The name had changed depending on which culture liked Homer's verse. The linguistic forms in Homer's stories proved that the main construction had been orally promoted around 800 BCE, long before actual writing had been invented. By 400 BCE Homer's books were written down in Greek script, but before that, the works were memorized and given orally by bards.

Donnie revisited inscriptions at Medinet Habu, where the pharaoh's battle was depicted. Several ancient galleys depicted sailors with horned helmets. Their many-oared ships had prows with bird heads, which differed from Egyptian ancient galleys. Ramses III was victorious, of course, as no Egyptian pharaoh would have recorded a defeat, only a great victory. Propaganda was nothing new to the ancients, but at least there had been a great sea battle at the appropriate time. It was, according to the inscriptions, against the Sea Peoples, who had raided and razed every significant settlement or city in the Levant. Ramses III was victorious after trapping the attackers as they entered the Nile where they could be attacked from on shore. Most of the warriors for the Egyptians were mercenaries, who often changed sides depending on their pay. Descriptions of the various tribes, some blond haired, some swarthy, indicated that some came from Sardinia, or further west. Others looked remarkably Greek with their clothing and hairstyles so different from the Egyptian forces.

Donnie knew that the Sea Peoples were an alliance of nine tribes. The Egyptian records listed them as "nine bows" and had various names for each of them. There were several depictions, each representing different weapons, dress, and methods of fighting. One group evidently used slings with rocks that killed opponents with a head strike. Others wielded axes, lances, swords, and there were several types of helmets. The tally of the dead was interesting, as Egyptians counted severed hands and phalluses, and categorized them circumcised or not. On the computer screen before him sailors were depicted with horned helmets. Donnie thought this must have been something he'd seen long ago, that his unconscious mind used now in his dream.

He'd forgotten all about this link due to his recent concentration on Scandinavians. That line of research had only brought criticism, or what he sensed was derision, even though their find was indisputable. Maybe his emotional brain was trying to divert his waking time to something more scholarly, or acceptable to superiors in the department. Publish or perish came with lots of pitfalls, and he certainly didn't want to jeopardize achieving full tenure. Achieving Associate Professor was the only thing that kept him from termination, after the "Viking" finds. Donnie decided to investigate the "Sea Peoples" and see where that would lead.

Right now though, he had to set the table and get the kids to breakfast. He smelled bacon, and knew there would be marmalade on toast for Sadie. That was her favorite, except for pancakes. He printed out the scene of the Egyptian battle to discuss with Val later.

"Wake up you sleepyheads!" called Donnie. As he entered the kids' bedroom, he saw that Andrew was already sitting on the floor by the bed, hooking up his remote-control cars.

"I'm being quiet, Daddy," said the boy sheepishly. Andrew really wanted his own bedroom where he could make lots of car noises or do pretend battles with action figures.

"You're a good kid," said Donnie softly. "Someday we'll get a bigger house. At least we have a big backyard and the tree swing. Maybe we can build a treehouse this summer. Would you like that?"

"You bet!" said Andrew. "With a trap door and a firepole too?" Donnie nodded, gave his son a hug, and said softly, "Get some clothes on. Mommy's got food ready."

Then Donnie looked at Sadie. She was surrounded with teddy bears. She smiled when she heard her daddy's voice. Soon they were all bopping to the table for a nice Sunday breakfast.

"What is that tune you are humming?" Donnie said to Sadie. Her mouth was full of marmalade toast, savoring the tartness of orange peel and jelly. She was visibly rocking and humming something new to her father's ears, something he hadn't heard before.

"I learned it yesterday at the festival," said Sadie. "We spent a lot of time at a booth where ladies were singing that tune, but I don't know the words. It was funny though."

Val then explained where they had been while her son and husband were off watching the heavy athletics. "We got corralled into singing at the 'waulking table' said Val. "They had spare seats around the table, and needed more people to do the demo. They were passing a loop of woven wool around the table from person to person, while singing. There were two empty seats."

"It was fun," said Sadie, "even though I didn't know the words. Part of it sounded like 'shane oh, shane oh.' That was the easy part."

Val smiled, and tried to explain to Donnie that the ladies were singing songs in Scots' *Gàidhlig*, the language of the Hebrides. "Remember when we were on Lewis? That funny sounding language."

"Right. But what was the demo about?" asked Donnie.

"We were told that when the wool comes off the loom, it is too loosely woven to be cut or made into anything, and it needs to be 'fulled' or tightened. They put the wool into a loop, dip it into a mordant, and push it around the table from person to person. The wool yesterday was dry, but in the actual method it would be stinky and wet. I hate to tell you what they used for mordant, but evidently the water from the peat bogs mixed with urine was very acidic." Val wrinkled her nose with the thought, as it was a big joke at the demonstration.

"So, they push it around while singing?" asked Donnie.

"We were told that the ladies bring the weaving they'd made during the winter, and that it takes many hours to get the wool fulled. You know in winter they have many more hours of night-time, nothing to do but weave their wool. But afterwards it's color-fast and waterproof."

"I'll show you, Daddy," said Sadie, as she grabbed the table-cloth with her chubby fists and shoved it back and forth in little spurts. Her little voice was singing 'shane oh', mimicking the song she learned. Val explained that the songs were mostly gossip, about any salacious thing that had happened during the long winter.

"Evidently the ladies would sing, and push the wool around all day, like twelve hours or more. Lots of daylight in the summer, you know. Didn't you hear the singing? I bet you could hear it a long way, except for the bagpipe noise. I think if the wind were still, you might hear those songs from far away, even if you were on a boat. But the bagpipe music was much louder and would sometimes drown out the singers. The ladies said once someone measured the distance that you could hear bagpipes, the record was forty-three miles away. I can imagine what it must have been like to hear Gordon's relief coming at the Battle of Khartoum. Bagpipe music is a one-of-a-kind sound. Anyway, the songs had lots and lots of verses, and we had great fun!"

After breakfast the kids went out to play in the backyard. Sadie had her little horses while Andrew raced his cars around the patio. Donnie cleaned up the dishes while Val put food away and got out some frozen left-overs for lunch later. Then they watched the Sunday morning news shows, read the newspaper, and laughed over the Sunday funnies. It was a perfect Sunday morning day of rest, though Donnie had some irritating thoughts about a meeting scheduled on Monday with his department chair. He enjoyed the distraction his family provided, and relaxed with an extra cup of coffee.

4

Through the outer glass windows, Donnie could see the chair-person's office door, closed, as usual. Donnie made sure he was on time, knocked and entered the outer office where the secretary sat intently watching the clock. Her reading glasses were perched on the tip of her nose as she followed the second-hand of the wall clock tick its way to the number twelve. On that precise mark she said, "You may go in now."

Donnie gave the door three light knocks, then entered and sat at the vacant chair in front of Dr. Harold Sturm's gigantic desk. The desk was devoid of any object except for the intercom and one lonely folder in front of the department chairman. No light came through the single outside window, as its opening was blocked by a huge metal bookshelf on casters. The room had a musty smell of being closed up with papers and books where no sunlight ever shone. Those shelves in front of the window held the accumulated production of each professor in the department. Shelves labelled by name included dissertation copies and other further publications. Each professor had a dedicated shelf, and all were full except for Donnie's. His shelf was near the bottom of the rack, dwarfed by all the others. One of his folders had a red dot on its spine.

The rest of the room was solid bookshelves, no other decorations at all, except for framed college degrees and awards earned by Dr. Sturm. Overhead, the fluorescent lights were unused. The room was illuminated by several floor lamps, and another one near the chairman's desk had a green glass lampshade. Donnie was uncomfortable with all this perfect organization. He imagined that every book and page number had been committed to memory by the man in charge of his career.

Dr. Sturm looked up as Donnie entered, glanced at the clock, nodded in approval. He straightened his already perfectly straight tie, then leaned forward, and with delicately manicured fingers, he picked up the single folder before him. Donnie's publication was titled "Insights and Comparisons of Egyptian Linguistic Forms between the 18th and 26th Egyptian Dynasties: Reassessing Methodologies and Assumptions" *Archaeometry*, Vol.38, no.12, 2004, by Morrison, Angus and Cameron, Donald."

"So, Don, would you like to encapsulate the insights you and Dr. Morrison have revealed in this publication? I looked at the synopsis, but haven't had time to comb through the fine print, just read the abstract. Of course, I'm not the linguistic scholar you are when it comes to hieroglyphics."

Clearing his throat, Donnie chose his words carefully. "The major problem we investigated revealed the lack of variation between any of the inscriptions. The letter forms and syntactical paradigms are exactly alike, although many centuries must divide their occurrence. The architecture is strikingly similar too, as if it were the same architect. Medinet Habu construction is a match for Kom Ombo. This should be impossible, given the assumptions of accepted Egyptian chronology and the fact that Kom Ombo was buried in sand and the same architect could not have seen it." Donnie paused, not knowing if he should attempt more clarification or leave it as is. Dr. Sturm's face was impassive, and to Donnie, unreadable.

"So, would you say that this publication is a good fit within the other research done in this department? I ask because I'm not sure your views are compatible with our conservative values in the field. Have you discussed this with anyone on the floor? Dr. Wilson perhaps?"

"No, Sir," replied Donnie. "There really aren't any other colleagues here as interested in the linguistic approaches that Dr.

Morrison and I have taken. Most everyone around here is doing Native American research. You might appreciate how difficult it is to establish any new approach in Egyptology with the essential difficulty of not doing on-site work. I have to rely on previously published research. This area of interest seemed perfect for exploring without actually being there. All these inscriptions have been carefully decoded many times over the last fifty years, so the results are accurate. Dr. Morrison and I are not questioning the translations, just the striking similarity in idiomatic and syntactical usages that shouldn't be there."

Donnie paused, then slowly continued. "It's as if they were composed by the same scribe but 300-500 years later. There are even instances of words that look convincingly like Hebrew, at least phonetically. However, two scribes separated by centuries would have different word usages, especially with certain deities being worshipped at such disparate times. These anachronistic idioms need to be explained. And . . . using an astronomical date for the accession to the throne for Ramses II is impossible. It couldn't be 1294 because of correct solar eclipse calculations. These discrepancies don't occur with other dynasties I've studied, especially given correlated contemporary records from other cultures." *His eyes are starting to glaze over,* thought Donnie.

Dr. Sturm stroked his grey beard, looked up and started to say something, as if trying to find something objectionable about the paper. He sighed, rather impatiently, then was quiet as if he seemed to change his mind. With a thin smile, he said, "I appreciate your close examination of ancient Egyptian writing forms, but explain to me why this is anything new? I'm satisfied that you have been published in a highly reputable journal, but what particular insights have you gleaned from this work?"

"It is new. But we did not come to a consensus or state an opinion on our findings. Dr. Morrison and I are hoping to receive comments from other departments around the world. It's more of an open door of inquiry for peer review, which might lead to upsetting the established chronology of Egyptian dynasties. Many have questioned Manetho's chronology before, and we expect others in the field to either corroborate our findings or dismiss them. Languages and their written forms simply don't stay the same through hundreds of years. The best explanation is that there is no actual gap between these dynasties. It is a major problem in chronology. We only want to uncover the truth, not cover up something that has bothered me for a long time. We hope to present our findings at the next Egyptological conference in Chicago."

Dr. Sturm sat with a level stare at Donnie. His face was emotionless, devoid of movement or interest. The chairman did not offer encouragement, or even a handshake. Then he stood, signaling that the meeting was over. "Thank you for your work, Don. We will wait and see what fallout might occur. Thank you for your contribution. How is the family?"

"Very well, Sir, thanks. We had an excellent time at a Celtic Festival in Springfield over the weekend."

"That's nice." replied Dr. Sturm with a smile. "I knew you were interested in Celtic rubbish." Then he glanced at the clock, and buzzed his secretary. "Thanks for dropping by."

Donnie left the office believing his meeting had gone well enough even with the verbal slight to his heritage. Still it was undeniable that the chairman seemed uninterested in the finer details of his work. It was like talking to some administrator who was only interested in publications that were uncontroversial. Angus and Donnie had published a new paper in a major publication, and though it was not entirely his own, it was good publicity for the university. Dr. Sturm had no grounds to think the paper was spurious, so why did Donnie feel so defensive? Research was supposed to be cutting edge, finding new aspects or information to the volumes of history. New chronology would upset the established timeline of pharaohs, but this wouldn't be the first time this had happened in academia. Was it the research or something more personal?

Throughout his childhood his red hair and freckles had labeled him in various ways, depending on the adult. Often he was viewed as "Dennis the Menace" just from a distance. Children his age would tease him sometimes, and as he learned to stay out of the bright sunshine, he did stand out in a crowd as being whiter than those around him. Donnie knew that as a child he often got himself in awkward situations, like petting a strange dog without asking or jumping down a flight of stairs without regarding the old lady before him. Having the extra-active mind of a kid who liked pirates and adventure, he fit the profile of the kid who couldn't sit still in the candy shop. He was leery of strangers and made friends slowly, so his treatment in the department didn't seem unusual for a while. Donnie wished he had some psychic ability that could tell him what the other professors thought of him. Maybe they just tolerated him as that weird geek who loved hieroglyphics.

Would it always be this way? Feelings like walking on eggshells or uneven ground was uncomfortable the longer he lingered and stood there. Donnie had chosen his words carefully and had the prestige of Dr. Morrison standing with him. That should be enough to keep his professional position. But Dr. Sturm was less than cordial. Donnie wondered if the man was just as stiff with the others in the department, or if the secretary even liked working for him. There were really no other professors to talk with, they all seemed just as cold and businesslike as their chairman. Even the break room went unused as other teachers just kept to themselves with their noses to the grindstone. Once, to commemorate the birthday of Robert Burns, Donnie brought a tin of shortbread cookies to share. No one mentioned it. At most, he felt invisible in the department. Donnie didn't want to worry Val, but he was uneasy about being treated like cut bait.

5

The gate latch jangled as Donnie made his way into the front yard of his little rental house. The grass was tall, needed cutting. Grasshoppers jumped into the air as he passed by. The white picket fence wasn't very high, and could really use a new coat of paint. Images of Huck Finn and Tom Sawyer rose to mind, and Donnie thought it might be a fun activity for Andrew to paint the fence before school started. The boy would be entering a new school next month. Donnie hoped the new teacher would be as accepting of a boy with so much energy. Andrew loved race cars, and actually ran everywhere he was going. Not such a good thing for second grade, but Donnie was confident Andrew would do well. He was already a good reader, and even read books to his little sister for fun.

Donnie walked up the front path. He saw blooming dandelions and other weeds, and thought that would be a good chore for Andrew to dig up the dandelions as well. Val was waiting in the open doorway, her apron fluttered like the wing of a swan. He jogged up to her, gave her a loving kiss. The white fence symbolized a safe haven, and all that was valuable to Donnie was enclosed by that little picket fence.

"How did it go?" she asked, as she looked steadily at his eyes. His face was impassive, giving no clues. Then he nodded and smiled. Donnie did not want to worry Val over his sense of insecurity about the meeting, so he chose to brush it off and put on a happy face.

"What's for dinner?" he asked, then from the kitchen he heard the children's voices say, "ropes!" and "snakes!"

Val laughed and replied, "something Italian, with special breadsticks. Sadie's using sesame seeds and Drew's using poppy seeds. That way we can vote on which bread we like best. Always a competition you know." Sadie was rolling rather thick pieces of bread with her chubby hands, not getting much length out of pieces of dough. But Andrew was standing, rolling very thin strips of dough, then braiding them into long pieces, with bulbous heads. They were obviously having great fun helping in the kitchen. The dough was put on baking sheets to rise, sprinkled with the seeds, and would bake for a few minutes while the pasta boiled.

"I put the mail on your desk," Val said, "There's a letter from Angus. Dinner in an hour." She looked at her husband expectantly, and Donnie knew he had to say something at least.

"My meeting went okay, no problems," Donnie said, smiled at Val, and then walked quickly to find the mail. He was happy when he saw the letter, shoved a few bills aside, and sat in his recliner to read what Dr. Angus Morrison had to say. Angus, and Donnie's sister Alison, had been his saviors when he was found in that hospital in Gibraltar seven years ago. How lucky he had been, for without their intervention he'd probably still be there. His hospital bed had been labeled "Jerry Flotsam" because the doctor believed Donnie was an American by his speech. Somehow, he'd washed up on the beach, barely alive. Donnie shuddered at the realization of how fortunate he was to be found, and that Dr. Morrison had befriended him. Fate had somehow brought them together, two Egyptologists who loved ancient writing and history. What's more, the Scottish professor was no stogy academician, but a man clear-headed and easy going as a teenager.

Angus' handwritten letter on personalized stationery was apparently written with a fountain pen because of the deftly fashioned serifs in his script. The calligraphy spoke of class, pride, and fine Scottish scholarship at St. Andrew's. In the letter Angus shared some of their current findings, more grist for the mill, so to speak.

Ceramic tiles at Medinet Habu were evidently made by a team of Greek laborers because on the tiles' reverse, Greek letters bore the mark of the artisan who had made them. By having them marked and tallied that way, the artisan would be paid for his own production. But Donnie and Angus knew that the presence of Greek letters at this time in Egypt should be impossible. Although the tiles had flowery "Persian" motifs rather than Egyptian letters or animals, the tiles were clearly integral during the construction of the temple. They could not have been added some century later for decoration. The letters were anachronistic.

Greek alphabet letters began codifying around 800 BCE and writing became more or less standard by 400 BCE. So, the letters were blatant proof that the temple could not be dated at 1200 BCE. There is no way the Persian tile motifs could have been added to the temple at a later time because they were decorating internal walls. This was proof that the temple was constructed much later than archaeologists believed, but it was doubtful the Egyptians would dedicate a temple to someone who had been already gone for hundreds of years. The evidence was becoming overwhelming that the temple was not as old as was stated in the accepted chronology of Egyptian pharaohs.

The letter went on to say that Angus was well, he'd written another monograph which he would send to Donnie after editing was done. Since California was still on tap for a visit to Disneyland, Donnie thought it would be an excellent tangent to visit with Angus and his sister Ali, who didn't live too far from Anaheim. If only he could swing the money to make a grand vacation to see Mickey Mouse and the "Happiest Place on Earth." Sadie would be in seventh heaven to see Tinkerbell fly from the palace, while Pirates of the Caribbean would suit Andrew just fine. There were only a few weeks of summer vacation left, and this year, a vacation west would be an excellent way to start off a new schoolyear for the kids.

But there were several bills for the Cameron household in the stack of mail. Donnie's position as Associate Professor didn't provide enough economic security, plus he was more aware of his precarious position after his meeting earlier that day. The peer review could be negative. The Fall semester would keep him very busy, though he did have a promising graduate assistant to help with grades and busywork. He and Val were in agreement about not putting stuff on credit cards, especially an expensive trip like Disneyland would be. But there was one option coming up. With both kids now in school, Val might get a position at the anthropology museum if the hours would match their kid's school schedules. Lots to think about.

"Dinner's ready," called Val. Donnie hurried to set the table, while Sadie helped with the napkins. Pasta Primavera was an elegant but cheap meal, made special by homemade bread sticks. Soon plates were heaped with steaming pasta, while a basket of breadsticks sat within reach. The ones with sesame seeds were a little fatter than the ones with poppyseed.

"Try mine first," said Sadie. Sadie smacked her lips in obvious appreciation.

"Use good manners," said Val, "and don't be piggish."

Sadie smiled when Andrew said "oink." Donnie gave his son a "look" and everyone happily took second helpings of pasta. Donnie had one of each of the breadsticks, and took bites of one, then the other.

"These are both great! Next time make the poppy seeds on the bottoms and the sesame seeds on top. Then I can have both at once!"

The kids giggled, and knew the competition was silly. Donnie had won their hearts again, and then Andrew spoke up.

"Dad, can we get a dog? Even a small dog?"

"Well, son, you're old enough to train it and do all the work for taking care of a dog," said Donnie, "but we have a problem. The fence around our house is only three feet high. A big dog could jump it easily, even a small dog could get out. Though we don't have much traffic on our neighborhood street, the dog might get lost, or want to chase a cat into the street. We'd have to take precautions."

"And it isn't right to have a pet cooped up in the house all day while you're at school," added Val. I might not be home all day either, if I find a part-time job. We could afford a dog, but it's the taking good care of it that's a problem."

"Can we build a higher fence?" asked Andrew.

"There are zoning regulations about the height of fences," replied Donnie. "I don't think a caged area like a 'dog run' would be too expensive, but that's not fun for a dog. Even a small dog can jump a five-foot fence. What kind of dog do you want? Big or small?"

"I want a Scottie!" said Sadie jumping in. "Like the black ones we saw at the festival. He wouldn't eat much. Can they jump?"

Donnie laughed, picturing a little black Scottie trying to dig his way out of the yard. There would be holes everywhere. As a child he'd had a little fox terrier who could jump a five-foot wall, so he knew that breed wouldn't work either.

"What about a bigger dog, like a sheepdog?" asked Andrew.

"Those breeds need a lot of attention and exercise. They're like you. They like to run around and chase stuff, and have a herding instinct that keeps them from getting fat and lazy. You'd have to take the dog to a dog park and train him to behave. Like 'heel, stay, and come.' Probably have to pay for some lessons."

"Okay," said Andrew, "but at least he'd know not to run in the street."

"Well, whatever dog we could afford would need training. The Scotties were bred for digging, Sadie. Our picket fence would be no challenge for a Scottie. They were fierce hunters of badgers. I think having a dog is not on the table right now, unless we get a bigger house, and a bigger backyard."

The kids had sad faces after hearing all the arguments against having a dog. Val was about to suggest getting Guinea pigs when Donnie spoke up.

"Maybe a trip to Disneyland would be better right now," said their father, which was met with cheers all around. The kids couldn't believe their ears.

6

For a usually bustling coffee shop in California, this Mimi's was, oddly, nearly vacant. In a rear booth, Professor Angus Morrison waited for Alison Cameron to make her "Loretta Young" entrance. Their loosely scheduled yearly meeting was overdue, and this was her choice of meeting place. Angus looked at the menu, saw a variety of scones, but tea? He'd have to chance a teabag, as he hated even the smell of coffee. He tugged, then buttoned his Harris tweed jacket, straightened his tartan tie and waited impatiently for Ali to come. At least it was quiet and they could talk without needing to yell, so common in the usual noise of busy coffeeshops.

The door chimes jingled a greeting as Ali sailed in, still in pink yoga attire. Angus waved, and called "Coorie in!" She joined the elderly Scot, smiling, then slid into the booth and sat with one leg flexed. She would have taken a yoga pose but there wasn't really enough room. They were uneasy friends, brought together over a persistent unresolved dilemma and their concern for Ali's brother. When the waitress sauntered over, Ali ordered a latte, Angus ordered black tea and two blueberry scones. He pronounced this the Scottish way, which rhymes with "gone." The waitress began to correct him, then shrugged and said they were out of blueberry. Angus substituted current and the waitress abruptly left with the order. Within minutes she returned with a large carafe of hot water, cup with teabag already opened, and two currant scones. Ali smiled when she saw the steaming latte. There was the outline of a white heart floating on the top asking for attention from her lips. The waitress smirked as she put down the hot water as if it were worthless. Teabags didn't cost much, wouldn't earn much of a tip. Perhaps she also wanted them to order more than two scones. After general niceties, Ali got right to the point.

"Val phoned last week. Donnie's nightmares have certainly not dissipated, though he's tried just about everything except acupuncture. Tried hypnosis, no success. He experienced what sounded like 'lucid dreaming' but it didn't happen again. If only he could control his dreams like that, he would sleep better. The good news is that they're planning a family trip to Disneyland. Maybe it's time to tell him, when they come, what we know about his near drowning. Maybe we can frame it in such a way that he'll remember sending me the papyrus."

"Doubtful," Angus replied, "he should have remembered what he did by now. We can't tell him what we don't even know. He will be shocked, but I want the truth to come out."

"I agree," said Ali. "Well, if he hadn't been so easily fooled by those treasure hunters, he wouldn't have done something so illegal. But he always was lured by some pretty face, as if flattery was what he needed."

"That doesn't sound like the Don Cameron I have as a research colleague," Angus said with tinges of Scottish brogue. "I guess you might know more about his love life. He certainly seems to be a careful researcher no prone to bein' fooled. Are you sure he wasn't being unethical too?"

"Don't you remember how quickly he wanted to turn in those Roman coins he found at Penafiel? He could easily have pocketed them. I think my brother has always been honest to his profession as an archaeologist, even with those things he and Val found in Illinois. Don't you smear his name without knowing what really happened."

Then Ali calmed a bit. "I know how it looks."

"But why would he do work for some fly-by-night treasure hunters called 'Finders Keepers?' Their slogan was 'we find it, you keep it.' That's not what a reputable archaeologist should do. Was he in lots of debt?" Angus asked. "I mean other than college loans?"

"Not that I know of. I think he just got seduced by the thrill of someone paying for his excavations, and his love of digging in the dirt. His description of the girl leads me to believe he was definitely in love. Would have done anything to gain her affection."

"We know they used him. That's shameful, but no worth attemptin' suicide."

"Suicide! No way," said Ali. "I think they tried to kill him. Probably knew they couldn't fool him much longer. Probably threw him off some boat. I'd sure like to know how he managed to smuggle the papyrus to me without them knowing it. Don't worry, I still have it, safe."

"It came to you in a package of bath salts, as I remember. Do you still have the outside wrappings that say where it was mailed from?"

"No, didn't save that. I remember it was from 'Isla de la Banyettas' or something sounding like that. Like a place for baths. I was just hoping to get an explanation with a phone call."

"Did you handle it like I told you?" Angus replied.

"Yes, I used my kitchen vacuum sealer, and then put it in the safe deposit box. It's available any time you want to attempt to Carbon-14 test it. I know you'd like to reveal the truth about the princess, but without Donnie's knowledge? We'll have to come up with a story or tell him and let the chips fall." Ali's face clouded over. But she wanted to get a feel about how far Angus was willing to go. She waited to hear what he would say next.

Angus didn't nod an assent. He knew that wasn't what she meant, otherwise they'd have revealed the find a long time ago. Their efforts to shield Donnie hadn't helped his PTSD. Still, they agreed long ago that keeping the papyrus hidden would at least save Donnie's career. Ethical problems like tomb robbing wouldn't sit well with anyone in his profession, no matter how conned Donnie had been. Seven years ago, there was no way Ali could tell him what he must have done, and but she had persuaded Angus to wait until they'd found Donnie. She wanted to protect Donnie no matter what. Now she questioned which was more important to Angus: publicity or Donnie's career? Proof about an Egyptian princess? Silence hung in the air like the absence of life. Finally, Angus spoke:

"You have no idea how long I've looked for evidence of Scota. It's been a lifelong dream of mine to prove her existence. When you brought that to me, right then and there I should have reported it. Too late now. If you hadn't been so distraught, we wouldn't be in this predicament noow. Canna be helped noow."

Ali sipped her latte. She kept quiet, not knowing what to say.

"Donnie and I have published a paper together," Angus said, breaking the silence. "It should help wi' his publication quota, though the peer review might be scathing. I'm safe in my department at UCLA, they're very liberal-minded. They even like controversy. But not so in Bloomington."

"I understand," replied Ali. "What was so controversial about it? Could we use it somehow to bring in the papyrus problem?"

Angus dabbed at his mouth and pushed himself deeper into the booth. "There's been a long-standing problem with Egyptian pharaonic chronology. It's not as cut and dried as you might think, especially when you deal with other contemporary cultures and their histories of rulers. We have a body of correspondence between Persian rulers, ancient Hebrews, and even kings of Ethiopia. Hittite kings were always fighting someone. Sometimes these letters, which are now accurately translated, show discrepancies between timings of events. One Ethiopian king is even asking advice about 'which of the three kings am I fighting?' As if in certain periods there was more than one pharaoh of Egypt simultaneously."

"Is your current paper dealing at all with that lady named Scota?" asked Ali.

"Only tangentially. That name never appears in any Egyptian records. It must have been a nickname. All through ancient history, royals used many names, sometimes depending on which year of the reign it appeared and which holiday they were celebrating. Actually, Pharaohs had five names, plus a 'secret' name that would protect them from harm. So there's the birth name, throne name, Horus name, and they believed that even knowing or writing a name gave you power over the person. There is a significant problem with the name of Rameses III, as Donnie and I found." Using his napkin, Angus again dabbed at his mustache and beard, then teased the scone crumbs off the tablecloth and onto his saucer. He finished his tea and waved for the check.

"Don't let's go yet," pleaded Ali. "We need to come up with some sort of plan to undo the secrecy of what Donnie did. Can't you think of anything else?"

Angus momentarily closed his sky-blue eyes, then said, "You're right. We need some skeleton of a plan. What he was involved with was truly reprehensible. But it's no worth his life or his future. Unless he can remember what happened, or admit what he did, the only solution is to turn it in anonymously. I'm not going to claim that I found it, and how can you tell him you've kept it a secret? This should have been revealed lang time since.

"But he was so fragile. You saw the pathetic wreck he was in the hospital that day we found him. When was I supposed to tell him?" Ali started to tear up. She'd protected her brother all his life; now she might be responsible for ruining it.

"Maybe more research is the answer," Angus said. "He's had time to heal. At least we might get lucky, find some new references that would lead us to revealing the truth. I've researched it for many years, but maybe with Donnie's fresh viewpoint, and expertise with idiomatic glyphs, we'll find something. In the meantime, maybe go on the angle of his being in love with whichever lady lured him in?"

"I remember her name was 'Kemi', never heard a last name. I think he was totally infatuated with her beauty and black hair. Must have met him when he was at Boston U. He was a champion swimmer there, which may be the reason he survived that swim in the ocean. Maybe mentioning her name would be enough to jog some memory of why he was in Spain in the first place. I could tease him about his choice of women. Glad Val is a wonderful person! I doubt she'd be jealous of some prior love affair. We're so lucky she came along for the trip. I don't think it was just rebound that they fell in love and married. Funny how things turn out with them meeting by chance. Makes me want to believe there is justice in the world after all."

Ali reached for her purse, retrieved Val's latest letter. "Val says they've planned a trip out to see us. Dates aren't confirmed, but they should be here in a few weeks. We need to come up with some crumbs of a plan before they get here. Maybe we should just somehow tell Val what we think happened, get her take on it first. She only wants what's best for Donnie and the kids. She's not ready to give up on him at all."

"Let's think this thing through more rationally," said Angus. "In the first place if Donnie had sent that papyrus to me instead, I would have reported the illegal theft and not jeopardized myself. But when he sent it to you, our only objective was to find him! We can't go back on what we did. But I remember when we met Valerie in Spain, what a lovely lass she was, I mean full of integrity. We must tell her what we know though it might threaten a bit o' pride she finds in him."

Ali nodded, "I know."

Ali held her fingers up into the air like air quotes: "Or, we could somehow rebury the papyrus and 'find it' again." There was no one within earshot, luckily, but an observer might have thought she was doing sign language since her fingers were doing repetitive figures. And she was getting quite animated, with an exasperated expression on her face.

Being as honorable and true to his own values, Angus had difficulty even imagining such a scenario. "I'll no do that!" Angus sneered.

"Well, the papyrus was found inside something, wasn't it?"

"Sure, a sealed box or amphora would protect it these last near three thousand years. Artifacts such as amphorae are pretty easy to come by in the antiquity trade since they are so ubiquitous. Even an Egyptian one of that age. Sealing it back inside one, and 'finding' it either in Spain or Ireland might be accomplished, but that's still illegal." Fingers were flying around "finding" and "illegal" but Angus had even more concern on his face, and his eyes no longer twinkled.

"Is that some kind of wine jug?" Ali asked, trying to somehow deflect the Anger she sensed from the elderly man. She put her empty cup on its saucer.

"You would buy an amphora?" Angus became even more angry. "Aye, most small museums have a stash of them, a dealer can sell them honestly, though I wouldn't want the purchase to be traced back to me! Don't you dare! Now you want to conduct an excavation in Ireland, and 'find' it there under cover o' darkness? This is not Indiana Jones!"

"I don't care! Would the Irish archaeology ministry let you excavate some site?" queried Ali. She was determined to find a way out for Donnie.

"Verra possibly. If I funded the exploration, and used my credentials to request it, they might allow it. It's been a lang bother o' mine that the Irish have refused to excavate known sites there, believing the dead should be left in the ground. Even the place called Glen Scohene has never been excavated, and that's where the myths *say* Scota was buried." Angus nearly spat out the words, he was so insulted with Irish religiosity. "But that doesn't solve the problem of provenance. And I'll no do that either!" Angus grew more impatient and conflicted. His reputation was at stake here, though Ali seemed oblivious and only thought of her brother. If they weren't careful, it would be a disaster all around. His tea was cold, and Angus wanted out!

Angus cleared his throat, and tried to regain his normal calm. He turned the carafe over, hoping the waitress would see he wanted a refill, but she was not within eyesight. He really wanted Scotch. Then he slowly explained, "The papyrus must be returned to Spain, to establish its true provenance. Unless Donnie remembers enough to establish the find, it will just have to go down unclaimed. Provenance is absolutely important."

"So, that's stuff I never thought of," said Ali. "Val's an archaeologist, so she could help establish where he was digging. She knows all about Spanish Celtic stuff. She was the docent at that site where we first met. Remember, Donnie even found some Roman coins there, and she had no difficulty turning them in to the office, even though she didn't actually see him find them. She might be able to turn in the papyrus too, but I understand your objection. We don't know where Donnie actually found it. But, if we were able to 're-find' the papyrus, then Donnie could translate it again and get the credit for that, you'd get the credit for helping him find it, and the truth about Scota could come out."

Angus bowed his head and hunched over the table. His thoughts were racing through any plan he could think of, and he was severely conflicted. Ali was determined to do something illegal to help her brother. Angus would have no more of it. From moment to moment he shook his head, as if trying to throw thoughts left or right. Ali sat and fiddled with the sugar bowl, flipping the spoon up and down as if digging through ancient sand. She exerted all her persuasion, as if it were a long yoga stance. Her thoughts finally formed words.

"So first we have to explain to Val about the papyrus. When they come to visit, we need to get her away privately, and explain what Donnie did. Let her give some suggestions, but explain I'd like to re-bury it and 'find' it again. Or if you could get permission to dig in Ireland, I would give the rest of my inheritance to fund the trip. Afterward, maybe take us all to Ireland, then over to the Isle of Lewis to see your sister. Sadie is named after her, and your sister was so happy last time we were there. She'd love to meet that little pixie. How much would all this cost?" Ali was determined to put an end to Donnie's nightmares.

"Probably more than you have. Doesn't matter. We can't re-bury it. Stop with these useless ideas! Look, I want to get the papyrus revealed. If you agree we should tell Val and Donnie, he might be interested in a dig. I'll start the communications with Dublin for the permission to dig. But I'll no bury it anywhere since we know it was found in Spain. I'd rather drop it in the hallway for the janitor to find than be connected with more fraud. Who knows, maybe the Irish are more interested by now and we'll find evidence of Scota. I know a burial was found with a necklace of faience beads, about the right time period, at the hill of Tara. Donnie and I have more work to do on the chronology issues, that will never go away until we're both exhausted."

"So, we're agreed to show it to Donnie." Ali said firmly. "I'll have it ready for him to see before they leave from home."

Alison looked at her watch, nodded curtly, stood up and gave Angus a big hug. "You are truly the best friend ever. You've taken a huge load off my mind!" Like a pink butterfly she practically flitted past the table and out of the coffee shop. Angus gathered his briefcase and left a tip on the table. The teabag sat in the cup like a little black pillow, completely devoid of flavor. A sour taste coated his tongue, but he was determined to valiantly figure a way out, for both himself and Donnie Cameron. Clans might have rivalry, but in the end, they stuck together. And Angus Morrison was no quitter! He also would not break his vows as an ethical archaeologist.

7

Angus walked out into the bright California sun. He looked the street up and down. He couldn't decide which way to go at first, he was so lost in thought and angry inside. His Good Samaritan help so many years ago had truly put him in jeopardy. His adventurous spirit, to help Alison find her brother, coupled with his absolute glee in finding evidence of Scota, had put him in an untenable position. Now there were choices, none of which were easy. He could report the papyrus find and let the chips fall, on Donnie of course. If Ali managed to secretly bury the papyrus somewhere in Spain, its accurate provenance would be void. Could he wait for some other solution? He couldn't just stand there on the sidewalk.

Angus turned and walked to the parking lot, got in his car to drive home. The traffic was miserable as usual, but he sometimes did his best thinking while sitting behind someone's bumper. He put a CD in the slot and listened to The Corries singing their rendition of "Liberty." *By the cross oor Andrew bore, by the sword oor Wallace wore, by the crown oor Robert swore, tae win oor Liberty.* He broke into song, his fine tenor voice filled the car, and soon he found himself turning into his driveway. "Time for a wee bit o' Glenlivet." he mumbled. He checked the mailbox, grabbed what looked like the usual flyers, and stomped into the house.

Nothing of interest appeared in the stack of mail at first, but nearly hidden inside the various flyers was a thin post from Sadie, his sister. She always used the thinnest airmail envelopes to save on postage, and of course the letter took two weeks to come all the way from the Isle of Lewis. Fighting to keep his anger under control, Angus poured himself a wee dram, and settled into his leather recliner to read. Her thin lines of perfect penmanship brought instant echoes of sitting in Sadie's cozy Crofter's house.

"Dearest Brother" the letter started, "I am writing to say I'm in a wee bit of need. The arrangement with the tourist bureau states that they want to quit our partnership. I guess they need to cut corners, and though the arrangement with the tours to the Lew's didn't amount much benefit to me, it was enough to keep house and hearth. I'm no wantin' to head to the mainland, of course. But to sell the Black House might be the best thing to do. Don't think I'd get much for it though, as without the tourist money, there's no point in keeping it on. Mairi Mack passed on about a month back, and no other crofts are occupied now. It's right bleak, if you know how I mean. It would be a pleasure tae hae a visit, Angus. Love, Sadie."

"Shite!" swore Angus. Apart from the lack of internet connection on Lewis, he thought Sadie could have at least given a phone call. Angus checked his watch, eight hours difference? Middle of Summer, Sadie might not be home, probably out working the seashore. He'd have to call in her early evening, maybe wait four or five hours when it would be daybreak on Lewis. More worries and choices, Angus was not keeping his temper under control. Flexing his fists, he poured another scotch.

Keeping Sadie's Black House open for tourists and "Bide a Wee Bed/Breakfast" experiences on the Isle of Lewis had been Sadie's extra income for the past twenty years or more. Recently a new hotel on Lewis, built closer to one of the seven stone circles, made for a shorter walk for modern tourists. Keeping the old ways alive had been worthwhile to the Scottish Tourist Board, but modern accommodations would now have the upper hand. The peat fires and their smoky atmosphere would soon come to an end, especially with the expanded source of electricity. Huge wind farms and wave farms, coupled with Scottish ingenuity might make the island more livable, but would signal the end of the old ways.

Maybe this is the best thing. Bring Sadie to America? No, she'd never agree. She'd never adapt to the mainland Glasgow bustle, let alone California insanity. This would never do.

Angus put down his glass with so much force the sound echoed off the walls. The problem though, meant another trip across the pond which might become part of the puzzle piece. The mantle clock struck five. Should he go down to the local pub or raid his pantry? Angus opted for the distraction, an easy choice to avoid his own cooking. The Black Watch pub was a short walk around the corner, a comfortable place to share a meal with friends and listen to whatever group would be playing. They usually took requests, and it would feel good to bellow out a song or two before hitting his pillow. Besides, without that interruption of his racing thoughts, he might never get a wink of sleep.

A good band was playing, actually one guitarist and a guy on a squeezebox. If he listened sideways Angus thought the concertina had a drone like a bagpipe. They played the usual standards for being a Scottish venue. "Flower of Scotland" followed a good rendition of the "Skye Boat Song," songs that Angus' clear tenor voice joined in with harmony. Somehow singing a good Jacobite song always both roused his spirit and calmed him inside. Angus sent over a twenty as a tip for the musicians, paid his tab, decided it was time to head home. The problems in Scotland seemed unsurmountable, being a function of the new pushing out the old. Tourists would still visit the standing stones, but the Tourist Board is probably right that modern visitors really preferred modern conveniences not found in the Black House.

Sadie had a few more years under her belt than Angus, and though she loved living on Lewis, loneliness was sure to impact however many more years of living alone she could stand. Selling her property on Lewis wouldn't gain enough of a bankroll to put her up in some retirement home on the mainland, even with Angus' help. He knew of no such place on Lewis, though Stornoway, being a good-sized city, must have something appropriate. At least the Brits took care of the elderly. Sadie would never go on the dole, but with no children or other relatives to take over, Angus and his sister were really the last of their branch of the clan. *Maybe time to write the genealogy?*

Angus knew the Morrisons had more than enough history to fill a good-sized volume. Maybe Sadie would be interested in compiling all the old folk stories and write about whatever curious customs she could bring to life. At least there was still strong general interest in Scottish ways of old which managed to sell a lot of movie tickets. Ancient burial customs and ghost stories alone might be described orally, maybe even a video presentation? Maybe it would be best to bring her to America after all. At least in California there would be plenty of available movie industry wannabes that would make a film just for the experience. Angus imagined Sadie dressed in period garments, speaking with her clear Broad Scots dialect, describing a birthing in an old black "hoose." He chuckled at the image. Another thought sprang to mind, of Sadie giving *Gàidhlig* lessons. The language had nearly died out due to the Brits not allowing it on legal documents. An Islander could no longer write "Kaithlin" on a birth certificate for instance. It had to be in English, written "Kathleen." The language, being as difficult as possible with its odd syntax, was just as much related to Basque as Irish Gaelic. Sadie, as old as she was, would be the last of the few natural born speakers, and therefore might be valued as human treasure. Angus mulled over all sorts of scenarios. He knew they would have to choose the best option, and face the problems of living into old age. Angus walked home, thinking about turning his guest bedroom into a home for his sister. At least she'd enjoy the warm California weather, if not the traffic.

8

The next evening Angus got Donnie on the phone, guessing the kids would be in their beds because of the time difference between California and Illinois. Angus mulled over the information germs he hoped to infect into Donnie's thoughts. It was time to start the Rube Goldberg ball rolling through the mouse trap game that might lead them out of the dilemma. He slid smoothly into his recliner as if he was entering a marathon. With pad and pencil nearby, glass and bottle within reach, he dialed the phone.

"Hey Don, got a space to talk tonight?" asked Angus.

"Angus? Sure, I've been thinking of giving you a call. Great minds think alike and all that. Good timing. Fire away."

"Was wondering if you've ever come across mention of that Hebrew judge, Samson? Seems like the city of Shemesh, south of Lake Tiberias was mentioned in some references at Medinet Habu, stuff I came across just recently," began Angus.

"Yeah. He was a Danite, 's-m-s-n,' is mentioned in one panel where the scribe was talking about alliances. Correlating with the Old Testament puts his dates at 1200 BCE. What made you think about that?" asked Donnie.

"Well, the tribe of Dan was one of the nine tribes of Sea Peoples named by Ramses, at least the timeframe is right for Samson. But Medinet Habu construction doesn't correlate. Glad I wasn't just imagining that. I've been wound up over some problems with my sister."

"Uh Oh? Sadie? I hope she's all right. Such a fine lady, she showed us such superb Scottish hospitality when we were there."

"She's fine, no worries. She's tough as an ox, good Scottish genes" chuckled Angus. "Just problems wi' the Tourist Board, and I think she's lonely because the last one of her neighbors has passed on. The government isn't going to support running the Black House any longer, which pretty much was her stable income. I'm thinking of takin' a trip over, but no plans yet. Eventually I need to make a better living situation for her. She'd love being your nanny for your kids. How's everyone at your home?"

"We're running ragged some days with the kids, but everyone's happy and healthy. The kids are wanting a dog, even two, but our house and yard aren't right for pets. The picket fence won't do, and I can't see dogs closed up in the house all day. Last week, Sadie found a baby bunny in the yard, must've squeezed through the fence. She had fun feeding it some lettuce, Anyway, to make the kids happy I tossed out an idea to go to Disneyland. So we might be coming out your way to visit Allison. At least Val and I have talked about a trip to the Magic Kingdom."

"Wow! Brilliant!" said Angus. "The kids would love that. You be sure to let me know so we can get together, aye?"

"Of course. What else is happening with your research?" asked Donnie.

"A colleague just released a paper on two queens interspersed between Akhenaten and Tutankhamun…have you heard that theory?" asked Angus. It was the wrong time period but useful to the path Angus had devised.

"Oh yeah, it's been all the talk in my department. One lady was probably the daughter of Smenkhkare. The other girl in the iconography is probably another daughter. At least that's what I thought, seeing her posed with 'caressing the chin' on the stele. Seemed like a standard adoration pose rather than sister stuff, as if they were even co-regents. Could be Meritaten. What do you think?"

"Aye. Tutankhamun would have been too young for the throne then, maybe they needed the teenaged girls to keep the dynasty afloat. Seems like plague period problems, too. So, have you found any other nicknames for either of those ladies?" Angus paused, then asked, "The name Scota hasn't popped up, for instance? I've been reading some spurious Irish myths that talk about a missing queen or princess from Egypt."

"Hmmm. Scota. Doesn't ring any bells. I did see some other pseudonyms connected with those princesses. Guess I wasn't really interested due to the time period. They must have been much later than our concentration you know."

Angus sighed, inaudibly. It was too hopeful that Donnie might instantly recognize the name, and Angus knew that. "It's Scota or maybe Scotach. Do keep an eye out for any references to that or other nicknames. You're good at keeping track of all their festival names. With the time discrepancy we're finding, this could be part of the solution. The amount of discord and upheaval during those times reminded me of the Celtic invasion documents, ever read them?" asked Angus. "I'm talking about the Tuatha Dé Danann."

"Nope," answered Donnie. "Send me what you have, there might be a connection with the Danites. Sounds like the same root name, tribe of Dan. People certainly got around more in those days than we give them credit for," chuckled Donnie. "Maybe they're one of the lost Hebrew tribes? That *Gàidhlig* language sounds a lot like Hebrew if you listen sideways." Even though his basic knowledge of clan lore didn't extend much into the Irish connections, Donnie was tickled with the thought.

"Well, we know the order of successions can't be accurate even with DNA research on those mummies. There was just too much intermarriage and incest. Just think about that weird name, Scota. Let me know if you run across it," repeated Angus.

"Absolutely, will do. Those Greek letters on the tiles are our best evidence so far though. Anything new found at Kom Ombo?"

"Not that I've heard. They still have time on their dig though pretty soon the heat will close it down. I'm anxious to go over, for sure, even out of season," said Angus.

"Me too! Wish I was independently wealthy. . . I'd go in a heartbeat. Politics are bad for Americans, though. Wish I could afford some C-14 tests on other things too, as unreliable as it is. My department won't provide much of anything these days. Maybe I'll zero in on Disneyland instead," quipped Donnie.

"Aye. Let me know the minute if you could swing a trip out. Maybe buy a lottery ticket or two. Might be that yer luck at finding artifacts could extend to picking lucky numbers. In the meantime, I'll scrounge my department for some coupons."

Donnie smiled. Yeah, Angus could be right about that, he'd always been lucky at finding stuff. But mostly pennies. Friends teased him about it, but, as an archaeologist, he was always looking down at the dirt. Donnie had a sense of pride knowing he was the best "finder" of his family. "Thanks again for your support. It's good to hear from you, Angus. I'll keep that name in mind, of course. You keep in touch and stay out of traffic. Who knows, maybe we'll be seeing each other soon."

"Aye, time for a wee dram," said the Scot. "Have a good night. Bye now."

Angus set the phone in its cradle, reached for the nearby bottle, and poured himself a dram. No ice, he liked it "neat" and it felt smooth as the scotch swirled over his teeth. *Uisce beatha, water of life,* he thought. No wonder Scots of old had whisky at breakfast, shunning tea.

Outside the wind had kicked up. Santa Ana winds brought heat to the valley instead of cool nights. The area had been in a serious drought, the farmers were all in trouble, and agricultural pickers had all been sent home. Even the strawberry crops were struggling these days. The miller moths had loosed their infestation since there'd been no rain. But California could weather the drought, unlike Egypt of old if the Nile flood was late.

Angus contemplated the fates of pharaohs when the river didn't bring its bounty. And the various plagues that were mentioned. Hard times for the people, it must have been a terrible challenge when the combination of invaders and pestilences descended. The climate had cooled, drought caused massive crop failure and there were strangely colored sunsets. The Hyksos kept invading, and records told of darkness in daytime and rivers running red. Ramses II wasn't titled "Great" for nothing, because he had met challenge after challenge and saved his country. Much like Nectanebus II would do six hundred years later. Still, the Tempest Stela records misery, privation and disaster. Corpses floating down the Nile, tombs flooded, and darkness during daytime. Eventually Egypt fell to invaders.

His daily news feed from Egypt said that an old cache of mummies that seemed destroyed by tomb robbers, was now decided to be hundreds of plague victims. Robbed of their burial artifacts they were beyond identification. And without names, they couldn't go to Amenti. Names, even the secret names, were of ultimate importance to the ancient Egyptians. Which is why so many statues had their names and titles effaced, or noses broken off. Even remembering a deceased person, and calling out their name, gave them strength in the afterlife.

Angus' and Donnie's research of the inscriptions had brought a sense of being in ancient Egypt. Seeing the hundreds of funeral portraits brought the dead into a feeling of knowing them, and how they lived. It was the immediacy of the situation. Angus hoped that Donnie would be able to find even more support for their theories, eventually make a breakthrough. The clues would be in the hieroglyphs, and Donnie was a master.

Angus thought how fortunate it was to have this friendship and Donnie's expertise. As he sipped his scotch, Angus felt their collaboration would earn success in academia. Donnie was so adept at deciphering even the most jumbled hieroglyphs and had made sense of even the most confusing iconography that Angus believed their partnership would steer them to the truth about the stolen papyrus. At least it was worth the gamble. He hoped that putting the name of Scota out in the open would tweak some lost strand of memory for Donnie, even in dreams. If he could only remember where the papyrus was found or any detail of his time in Spain, it would be worth the effort to jog his memory. But not risk his academic position. If Donnie could not remember on his own, Angus vowed he would be the last person to put himself or Donnie in jeopardy. As much as he wanted to prove the Egyptian connection to Scotland, Angus could stand the wait one more week. After all, he'd waited most of his life to prove his theory and somehow, he believed, it would eventually happen.

9

"Mommy, Mommy!" Sadie yelled, running into the house. "The bunny's back. Come see." She grabbed her mother's hand and pulled her out the door. Sure enough, the little brown cottontail sat in the middle of the vegetable garden. His little nose twitched as he munched the tasty lettuce leaves. He had come back through the fence, maybe hoping for more sweet lettuce or a carrot top to munch.

"Can I feed him again?" she asked Val.

"I suppose we can spare some more lettuce. But what if the bunny learns to get food here?" Val paused and considered the best way to encourage her daughter to think about choices. She really wanted the kids to have the responsibility involved with pets, but Donnie had nixed having a dog. It seemed the rabbit would fit the need. "The bunny might decide to stay if we keep feeding him. What might happen?" said Val.

"Oh, you mean he might get fat?" said Sadie.

Val giggled. "Well not fat, but he will grow. Maybe get too big to squeeze back through the fence. His mommy would be so sad without him. She might not miss him for a few mornings, but what if he didn't go home? Do you think the mommy rabbit would miss her baby?" Val waited patiently for Sadie to make her choice.

"Ok Mom, I'll just watch the bunny and see what he does. Maybe he'll go home if we don't feed him. But I think he will eat the nasturtiums instead," said Sadie.

She was right. The little cottontail continued hopping through the flower garden area, munching on succulent leaves and flower petals. The rabbit wasn't the least bit intimidated by the nearness of the little girl, didn't even hop away fearfully when Sadie reached down to give it a pat on the head. He just quietly munched a cheek full of green leaves and wiggled his little fluff of a tail. The bunny, interested in selecting tasty leaves, seemed oblivious of being in any peril from the little girl watching him.

Sadie sat nearby, wondering what she should do. *If we feed it, it will stay, but if we don't feed it, Mommy's flowers will be eaten.* Sadie clapped her hands in warning as the rabbit moved closer to the daisies. This startled the bunny. It looked up, as if understanding that the daisies were off limits. As Sadie got to her feet to come close again, the bunny hopped away to a corner of the fence area, and suddenly was out of sight!

Sadie went to the spot, and found a hole. The rabbit had dug an exit, concealed by some weeds, and would be able to come and go between the pickets. *Oh, the bunny can go home.* Since the size of the rabbit was not a problem anymore, Sadie walked happily back into the kitchen, looked in the refrigerator, and found a small carrot. She triumphantly took that carrot back outside and laid it in the grass near the bunny's hole. Then she sat down some distance away to see what would happen.

Sure enough, the rabbit emerged. The soft little nose twitched, soon found the carrot, and the carrot disappeared into the rabbit's bulging cheeks. Sadie would have a pet!

That evening as the family was sharing a pizza, Sadie said, "I have a secret friend. I've named him 'Noses'."

"Does this friend wiggle his nose like this?" said Donnie as he made his nose muscles wiggle his nose up and down. Everyone laughed, but Donnie just continued to wiggle his nose. Then he pretended to bounce in the chair, and he put his fingers on the side of his head like ears. "Am I your secret friend?" he asked Sadie.

"Oh Daddy, you're silly. My new friend is the bunny that comes to visit me in the back yard. He's not scared of me at all, and he can go home whenever he wants to."

Donnie stopped his antics and nodded. "Ok, how does he do that?"

"There's a bunny hole under the fence," Said Sadie, and I'm the only one who knows where it is. It's a secret."

"Goodness gracious!" said Val. "That's why my flowers look so ragged. I thought we had a gang of caterpillars or grasshoppers. That's ok, maybe you should feed the rabbit some lettuce, and Daddy can put up a little fence around my flowers." She sent an inquiring glance at Donnie.

"It won't do much good to fence off the flowers 'cause bunnies can jump or dig," said Donnie. "And I don't think a fence would look very nice around the flowers. Soon Mom won't have any flowers left if we don't shoo it away."

"I thought it would be an easy choice for a pet for the kids," quipped Val. But she wasn't happy. *The trip to Disneyland is a great idea, but when that's over, we'll be back in this tiny house on the prairie . . . and, I'll be sleeping on the couch most nights.* "It's your turn to clean up the kitchen," said Val quickly. "I have some paperwork to do, you know mommy is looking for a job."

Val left the kitchen in a huff. Sadie looked at her father, who simply stared at his wife as she left the room. Andrew began clearing the cups. "It's only a rabbit, Sadie. It's not ours, so forget it."

Donnie was startled at Val's outburst. Here he was focused on bedtime stories instead of what was right before him. The problem with the rabbit brought other thoughts to his mind. *Val isn't happy about going to work. I'm a terrible husband.* Sadie began to sniffle but at least Andrew didn't make fun of her. Most times he knew better than that.

"I think after dinner tonight we'll take a trip down the rabbit hole," Donnie said, as he forced a smile for the kids. "Help me with the paper plates and stuff, and hop into your jammies. We'll have an extralong story time tonight. Sadie gave a quizzical look, then giggled.

Donnie wiped the table as the kids finished their tasks and ran off to find their pajamas. The kids had already heard the stories about Mr. MacGregor's farm. *There are rides in Disneyland about Alice's Adventures in Wonderland. Maybe they're old enough now to hear the real storyline behind Alice's travels.* Always the storyteller, he wanted his kids to think, as well as enjoy the fables. He went to the bookshelf and easily found the volume, in its space after *Aladdin's Magic Lamp. At least my books are organized if my life is a mess.*

As the kids snuggled together with their dad in his big recliner, Donnie propped the book before them. "Down the Rabbit Hole" was the first chapter. He began to read quietly but was interrupted almost immediately by his daughter.

"That's funny," said Sadie, "my rabbit's hole is too tiny to go into. And Alice's rabbit is talking."

"That's right," said Donnie, "so this is imagination. What would you see in a hole in the ground?'

"I'd see bugs and worms," Andrew stated. "It would be cool to get all dirty, but I'd want a ladder to get back out." Donnie knew his son was a risk taker and laughed. Sadie frowned but would have been happy to follow her brother anywhere. Donnie knew that as when he was a child, both of the kids would dive in head first out of curiosity.

The children listened to Alice's adventure and the description of what she saw on the way down, her skirt acting like a parachute slowing her descent, and shelves of marmalade. The kids laughed from time to time with the images the author had conjured up. When Donnie came to the end of the chapter he stopped for a discussion. There was lots to talk about, not just warnings about drinking from suspicious bottles that could have poison, or being late to a party.

"One of the first things to know about this book is that the author uses a fake name, like a nickname," said Donnie. His name wasn't Lewis Carroll but Charles Dodgson, and he was a college teacher like me. I think he liked having a nickname."

"Oh, that's like Dr. Seuss." Said Sadie. "I like being called Sadie," she said smiling, "but Mommy told me they would probably call me Sarah when I start school."

"Well, it's just like you say 'mommy' instead of Valerie, and I'm called 'Donnie' instead of Dr. Cameron. Almost everyone has a nickname or a title. You know Dr. Seuss wasn't a doctor."

"Do I have a nickname?" Andrew asked.

"You could be either 'Andy' or 'Drew'," Donnie replied. "Do you like one better than Andrew?"

With a quizzical look on his face, Andrew said, "Neither. I like my name like it is."

"That's fine, Andrew. I just wanted you both to know about nicknames. I have an important search for a nickname with my work stuff. Sometimes people have other names to cover up secrets. Sadie named her rabbit 'Noses' 'cause that fits. I think Andrew fits you just fine."

"In the story Alice starts falling," added Donnie, "but then slows down. If you fell in a hole like that, you wouldn't slow down. But this rabbit hole is supposed to go all the way through the Earth, like supposing you could dig your way to China. Two hundred years ago people thought you could drill that far. But if you got to the center of the Earth, air pressure and gravity wouldn't let you come out the other side. That's why Alice slows down like an elevator. Now science tells us it would take forty-two minutes. Mr. Carroll did the math to prove it, but forty-two is a special number. When you're older, I'll explain that, too." The kids were quiet, so Donnie asked another important question:

"So would you take a drink from a bottle that said 'drink me'?"

"Nope," said the children in unison. "But it would be fun to shrink down tiny," Andrew added. "But only if I could grow up again. I want to be big and strong like you, Dad." Donnie felt a sigh of relief, knowing that neither of his kids would drink something out of curiosity, or even peer pressure. Every story was an opportunity for raising smart, safe kids, even in their small town in Illinois there were dangers.

Donnie talked about a few other things in the chapter and the kids laughed about Alice's predicament of being too big for the white rabbit's house. Donnie thought he should build Sadie a doll house but he had no time. *Time! I have so little time to do stuff with my kids. And summer's almost over. The next semester would be a grind, too.* By now it was bedtime. Donnie tucked them into their beds, and with kisses goodnight, went to look for Val. Donnie felt confident that the stories were well worth telling, and that again he had done his best at being a father. Though he wanted more income and a good savings plan for two sets of future college costs, at least his kids would remember story time and the priceless gift of love.

10

He found her sitting on the porch swing outside, iced tea in hand. With the stifling night air, it seemed the heat of the day would not lift. She seemed to be intently listening to the crickets, counting the seconds, and estimating the temperature. She had at least finished a lot of paperwork. "Kids asleep?" she asked when she saw Donnie on his way over. "I'll go tidy up."

"Oh Val, it's done. Please let's talk. I can put up a fence to save the flowers from that rabbit if that would make you happy," Donnie offered. Then he asked, "Are you mad at me?"

"No," Val replied. "Maybe. . ." Val hesitated, not wanting to vent her hidden feelings. "It's jus' that our tiny rental is driving me nuts. The kids are growing. They shouldn't have to share a bedroom for one thing. But it's more than that. We are barely making ends meet. Part of my worries are about our trip, but even without that expense, they need to pay you more. We aren't saving anything. And I don't want our kids to have huge college loans to pay off." Val paused, not knowing if she should continue. She didn't like to complain. Then she thought to take the plunge.

"I thought associate would be more secure, but you keep writing controversy. Angus doesn't have that problem. It's like you are purposely pissing the department people off." She wiped her eyes, took a deep breath, and continued. "And, I think kids need to learn responsibility by having pets. Things are just bugging me tonight. It's nothing new, but the stupid paperwork and the heat. No biggie." Val sighed and gave Donnie a hug. Secretly she didn't want to take a job but it was obvious to her that going to work would solve most of their financial problems. "I didn't mean to dump on you, sweetheart. Maybe I'm just hot. I love you no matter what."

Donnie nodded. "Yeah, you're right. I like the heat though. I like getting dirty and smelly. Maybe I like sticking it to the academic stodginess. It's a risk, but life is full of risks. Things will get better, I promise. The work I'm doing with Angus should bring some speaking engagements, maybe a book sale. They can't be too critical, and if it's as well-received as we hope, I'll be sure to get a raise. Won't it be great to see Alison? The kids are so excited about the trip. A change of scenery will do us good you'll see."

Val stared momentarily, being quiet. She thought ignoring the problems might be how Donnie managed most of the time. She looked at him quietly and said, "I don't think a trip will be enough, though. Get real! You are still having nightmares, and even though California might be cooler, I'm still afraid to sleep with you. Alison has only one extra bedroom, and the kids will have to sleep on the couch or living room floor. Renting hotel space will be too expensive, and anyway Ali expects us to stay with her."

Donnie grabbed his head as if he could squeeze out some poison. He bent over on the swing saying, "I know! I know. . . nothing has worked. I hate myself for these night terrors. Maybe I should just not sleep at night, at least not in bed. Make myself uncomfortable until I'm too exhausted. Or get drunk." Donnie began to cry like a little boy who had lost his best friend. At least that's how he felt. He wiped away a few tears in embarrassment.

Val put her arm around him, and they began to rock in the swing. She began humming a little lullaby and soon had Donnie's head in her lap. She tried to console him but he continued sobbing. Hot wet tears stained her jeans, but eventually Donnie calmed.

"I haven't bugged you about this lately," said Val, "but I just see problems ahead with the trip. Meds haven't helped, and I certainly don't want you to drink. All I know is that when we met you were like a blank slate. You have come so far in . . . I don't know, in living, but it's like you've hit a blank wall with the nightmares. Alison told me that you had gone to Spain with a girlfriend. A woman named Kemi. Do you remember that?"

"Some girl? Hope you're not jealous," Donnie teased. "No, and I've really tried. All I can piece together is that I was on a dig in Spain, though of course normally my interest is in Egyptian finds. Makes no sense. I know Egyptians did mining all over, even in what is now Spain, but so did the Phoenicians. It's impossible to tell if Egyptian artifacts found in places like that were just trade goods, or were from Egyptians living there. It's like finding something in the attic that could be an heirloom, or only made to look antique. You don't know if it's contemporary or old."

"I know from my work in Spain that we'd find Roman pottery mixed in with other stuff that seemed much older. Aren't there other tests to do these days?" Val asked. She really wanted to know about that girlfriend so she played along, kept him talking, hoping to bring up the girlfriend thing again.

"Sure, but we can't rely on radiocarbon tests. Even the ship called the Uluburun that sank off the coast of Turkey might not be dated right. Archaeologists date its sinking at 1300 BCE. The ship was about fifteen meters long would have carried twenty tons of cargo. Many of the swords on board came from Northern Europe because they were cast, not forged. The ship carried lots of metals, mostly tin for making bronze, but also gold scrap, including one piece stamped with the cartouche of Nefertiti. We've still not identified her mummy, though the whole Valley of the King's area was subject to thieves who could have stolen it. When they broke into a sarcophagus, they would rip apart the mummy wrappings, looking for gold. Many mummy parts got mixed together and left as garbage."

"Egyptologists haven't identified the mummy of Nefertiti. She could be the 'Older woman' mixed in with others, but even DNA is inconclusive. That piece of scrap gold would have been fifty years old by the time of the shipwreck. Other things on the boat, such as stirrup jars, look more modern, closer to 1200 BCE or so because they're inscribed with the Greek's Linear B. So which date should we believe? It may be a hundred years newer than the accepted date. And we don't know why the ship sank. . . could have been a storm, pirates, or caught in some sea battle. The battle of Troy is dated to 1186, could have involved that ship."

Why is C-14 so unreliable? I thought that was the gold standard for stuff," asked Val.

"The radiocarbon test works only on organic stuff, as you know, although researchers can identify a stone's quarry by the isotopic proportions. Getting a date of when the stone was carved is unlikely, 'cause that depends on the stone's 'varnish' or exposure to the climate, even pollution. So we can use C-14 better on wood but it's still not accurate. Usually the wood on the boat was made of planks from the outside layer of the tree. Unless we can count tree rings, the wood planks could be extremely old. Depends on how long the tree lived before it was turned into a boat. Oars found could yield a different date.

"What's more, researchers find different values depending on whether the artifact is northern or southern hemisphere. Evidently the Thera eruption and the subsequent Santorini destruction caused so much ash and carbon to be layered in places that the decay levels don't correlate accurately. After all, dating the olive branch buried in ash with the Thera eruption has made a younger sequence with other wood, making a significant range in the data. Even when they date the wood in Tut's tomb, it's hundreds of years older than the flax mats and linen pillows. All those dates need to be revised. Maybe Thera wasn't 1600 but closer to 1200 like the historical records describe."

Valerie tried to steer Donnie back to her subject. Not that she was jealous of some past girlfriend, but Ali had been insistent that it would help. "Yeah, but Spain? What were you doing there? Living with some chick?"

Donnie threw up his hands in frustration. "A girl? Ali always warned me about my dating choices until you came along. She hated all my girlfriends. Thank goodness she likes you. . . But I used to have vivid dreams about an Egyptian goddess, like Maat, not a real person. I used to try to ask her questions in my dreams, about her laws and stuff."

"Laws? Oh, like how to pass through her judgment?" asked Val.

"Yeah, funny thing. I was telling the kids tonight about Alice and the rabbit hole and got into a discussion about falling through the earth. Lewis Carroll was a great mathematician, so he was really giving a scenario about physics. That funny number forty-two keeps coming up. Did you know that Maat had forty-two laws to weigh the heart with. . . on the scales?"

"Ok, I know, that October goddess. Do you think you broke some laws? Maybe some kind of guilt is causing your amnesia. Did you dump the girlfriend? Ever dream about her?"

"You have no reason to be jealous of someone I can't remember," Donnie retorted. "I only remember black hair. Maybe she was an Egyptian. Of course Ali thinks she was bad, even a criminal . . . why, I don't know." Donnie sat up, shook his head, and hugged his wife. He stopped the swing with his feet, as if making a stand. He became assertive.

"You've been so patient. I need to find other professional help. I promise to get this resolved before we go to Disneyland. Maybe there's a sleep clinic that could record my nightmare mumblings and I might talk out loud. It's like I did something wrong. Maat is judging me, but I don't know why. You know I was drowning in most of it." He shook his head, then said gently, "Thanks for loving me." He started to leave, thought better of it, and sat back down on the swing with Val. They sat together without talking until the moon set. Then they went to the bedroom and made love in the hot Illinois night. Exhausted, they both slept soundly. For Donnie, it was the first time in a long while that he slept with his wife by his side.

11

Donnie prepared for an extended wait in the muted light and subdued music of the psychiatrist's office. He closed his eyes and folded his hands, as his previous visits to doctors had strained his patience. If he had ever kept students waiting like this, they would just up and leave. But Donnie had solemnly promised himself to end his nightmares, no matter how long he had to sit. Although he'd slept well last night, the excellent sex had something to do with that, and he was exhausted from staying up so late. Right now, he was mostly tired of the dozens of pages of questions, filled with the best answers he could remember. Questions, like whether or not he had a dog or a cat as a child, seemed senseless to Donnie, nor did he ever chew his fingernails. But he'd done all that he was asked to do, so that the doctor couldn't possibly find any more time to waste. His experience with psychiatrists proved that they were good at smiling and nodding. That way patients would make multiple trips and have extensive medical bills.

He was hoping this would be his last visit to a psychiatrist, but experience taught him that shrinks liked to take their time. He hoped this doctor would be different. Before he could doze off, he heard the receptionist call his name.

He jerked to attention as Dr. S. Cohen was suddenly before him. She ushered him to a soft chair in her sunlit office. Behind her desk hung the usual certificates and licenses, which revealed her first name as "Sundance." *Hippie parents* thought Donnie. He hadn't noticed her first name before since it wasn't on the letterhead. She was dressed casually in slacks and a blue blouse, a light blue jacket hung over the back of her chair. The potted plant in the corner looked suspiciously like a hemp variety. Donnie was distracted, then saw a thick folder holding details of his previous visits, as he had all his files from other doctors sent to her. He wanted to cut to the chase. The additional various personality tests and protocols he'd filled out seemed totally unconventional to say the least. But Donnie was determined this would be the last therapist he'd ever visit.

Her desk held this main folder, plus other endless protocols Donnie had completed. Sitting in one corner of the otherwise spotless teak desk was a small paper box, about three inches square. Each side had vistas of blue sky and clouds, but Donnie thought it must be a cover for something beneath, like some sort of toy. He really wanted to reach over and pick it up, but managed to restrain himself. Dr. Cohen observed this, and to quell his curiosity picked up the little box. Underneath was a replica 'heart scarab' so common in gift shops. Donnie recognized the trinket immediately; he could spot a fake a mile away.

"Just a souvenir from a friend of mine," the doctor replied. "When the world gets tough, I just cover him up, let him hide. I'm sure you are familiar with coping mechanisms."

Donnie nodded sheepishly, but realized she said it in a kind voice.

"I fully understand you'd finally like to resolve whatever is still upsetting your life, so let's not waste more time. Your previous diagnoses include closed head trauma, a near drowning, and generalized amnesia, but C.T. scans show no organic damage. Do you experience any physical weakness or numbness of hands, for example? Loss of oxygen in near drowning would show up with physical ailments.

"My body is strong. I exercise at the gym before work. But I won't swim in the pool. Still too scary, though I used to be a long-distance swimmer. Guess that's what saved my life."

The doctor nodded. "Without physical brain damage, we then have to assume a diagnosis of 'traumatic dissociative amnesia' or 'psychogenic amnesia.' On the one hand, your brain may be refusing to remember what led up to your near drowning. On the other hand, those memories may not even be recorded since you were totally attending to not drowning."

Donnie thought a moment before asking. "You mean my synapses didn't even record the event?"

"It's like being in an armed robbery and later asked to identify the assailant. You only see the gun and not the crook's face, so you can't identify him. But you do remember the gun. This is common. It says in the reports that you even lost your personal identity. How did you get home?"

"My sister and her friend came and identified me with missing person photographs, and the U.S. Consulate issued me a new passport on her affidavit that I am her brother. Most of my childhood memories returned, and I can still read hieroglyphs and do my work, but the amnesia and trauma of drowning is ruining my life."

Dr. Cohen made a few notes with her pen before smiling kindly at Donnie. "This massive repression of trauma is usually relieved by hypnosis or certain medications. You've tried only sedatives? How about anti-depressants or cannabis?"

"Meds haven't helped. Maybe I need truth serum."

Dr. Cohen sighed, still smiling. "If the memories are stored, we will unblock them. You need to trust me and believe that whatever we find will be confidential. My review of the personality protocols reveals certain of your personal constructs, meaning secrecy is important to you. I will keep your secrets. How is your sex life with your wife?"

"Satisfactory." Donnie didn't want to say "great," especially in July. He knew it was weird that his nightmares only happened in the July heat. Something bad had happened in a hot July, while he was in Spain, but mentioning that usually brought disbelief in therapists. It was just weird.

"How is the family doing, everyone happy?"

"They're being understanding and patient, but we need more money. Val is planning to find a job when Sadie starts school. I don't think she's cool with it though. The kids are always involved with something to keep them busy. You might consider them 'high maintenance.' We're a happy bunch, but they don't know about my nightmares. The kids want a dog but we don't have room. None of us want to consider having a cat. Why does it matter if we don't have pets?"

"I noticed in your medical records that both you and your wife are Rh-negative. The fact that you have avoided having a cat around is related to a parasite that cats carry. It's called toxoplasmosis, and virtually everyone in the world will have antigens to this virus. Except those of your blood type." Dr. Cohen raised her voice to add emphasis, so Donnie couldn't ignore what she was saying. She looked directly at him, then continued.

"Exposure, which is virtually unavoidable in the world, tends to cause certain behavioral patterns in a small minority of people. With your red hair, I would guess that you were a very active little boy, maybe even hyper? Statistics show risk-taking and a higher incidence of traffic accidents, for example. It's just one factor where blood antigens affect outward behavior."

The information came as a shock to Donnie but he kept a quiet face and demeanor. He wasn't believing some correlation between behavior and blood types, but thought maybe more research would be interesting. The behaviors she mentioned certainly did apply. Donnie remained skeptical though, and offered no comment.

Dr. Cohen waited, then continued. "Even small things can be used as blockages to the underlying problem. It's like fences around something ugly you want to hide. I understand hiding it from the kids. But evading my questions will not lead to progress. Problems with a mother-in-law or work?"

"None of that. I'm happy as I can be under the circumstances. It's just that I've been seen doctors before, many times, and I'm still screwed up. But there is a lot of pressure at work. Publish or perish stuff." Tears welled up in his downcast eyes as he told the doctor about their upcoming trip, and the urgency that had brought him to the realization that the status quo would no longer suffice. Val had never pushed him before, and though their love was strong, he told the doctor he sensed a breaking point. Donnie wanted to be as open as a child but it was hard to put aside his professionalism.

"I'm glad it's not another Rorschach," Donnie blurted out, "but your tests were like being in with the high school counselor. Personality tests?"

"I understand," the doctor replied, "but my methods will get results. I am a Cognitive Behavioral Specialist, which means I don't only look at behaviors, but the cognition behind them. Pavlov's dog learned to salivate on cue, but it couldn't act with the intelligence of a human being to resist it. Perhaps my reputation brought you to me? I've been measurably successful with what you might consider unconventional. As long as you are truthful and don't hold back anything, even things that seem trivial may be most important."

"Ok." Donnie was glad he hadn't insulted the woman. He told her about his July sleeping arrangements, how much he loved his wife and kids, and his hopes for the future. Dr. Cohen responded gently, made him feel accepted, and eased him into what would be her conclusions.

"You have an extremely high regard for honor and living within a code of conduct. This is tied to your profession, but it also imbues your mundane behavior. I expect your office is regimented, books are in perfect order, and schedules are kept promptly. You are never late, nor do you ever misplace or lose anything. You expect to find things where they should be, that is, everything has its place. Correct?"

"Right. But I don't expect this of others, certainly not my kids or Valerie. They can be messy, just not me. When I'm on a dig, it's methodical, step by step, so that everything is recorded in its place. Valerie was a great assistant on our Illinois dig, and she's a better artist when it comes to sketching the finds and strata. Just so you know."

"I fully understand your methods and behavior. That's why it's so hard for you to admit if something is lost or not recorded accurately. You mentioned that the recent paper you worked on with Dr. Morrison was about a chronology error connected with Egyptian records. This is another indication of how you feel mistakes need correcting. You have taken risks in academia to set the record straight as you see it. This is evident in everything you do."

"I can't have the world believing something I know is wrong. Even if I'm the only one trying to prove something. I'm lucky to have Dr. Morrison on my side."

"Well, that's the answer to your problem. Everything I know about you tells me that something happened before your near drowning, something connected to your professional behavior and reputation, that you can't admit happened. I suspect you did something so against your beliefs, that your mind refuses to admit it to yourself. Could you have been suicidal at the time? Drowning could avoid lots of problems, or guilt. What could you have done?"

"If I had stolen an artifact or damaged an archaeology site, or lied about something, maybe. . . that would do it. But I'm a professional. I wouldn't do any of those things! I would rather die than break the norms of my profession. I can't believe I did something like that, for any reason." Donnie shook his head and started to rise from the chair.

Dr. Cohen motioned for him to stay, directing him to a couch. In the dim light, he hadn't noticed it over by the bookcases. As he lay down the doctor's voice drifted to him, and he felt supremely comfortable. It was then that he noticed the smell of spicy incense of some sort. Donnie smiled, thinking at least it wasn't patchouli, more fitting for some grown up hippie. Dr. Cohen moved her chair so that she sat behind Donnie's head.

"Hear me out," said the doctor. "This will not be easy, but we will keep any secrets, as if they are merely a fantasy. Let's pretend it is a mystery story you might read. The more details you can imagine, the more it will affect you emotionally. Let's imagine a storyline with some clues. It's about an archaeologist who finds something golden. But he wants to keep it. Should he steal it or hide it from the authorities? Maybe it gets stolen from him and the cops are after him. Let's do this now. Close your eyes."

The doctor's voice became soothing and hypnotic. "Imagine yourself on a dig in Spain, in a secluded area. You are not alone. These things are not done alone. Right? It stands to reason that someone is with you, someone you admire or respect, who was significant in your life. So significant that you might harbor a suggestion you otherwise would not consider? Remember, this is just an emotional construct, like a pill you must take. Trust me."

"But this is fake! It's like a movie, but you want me to be in it, even if it's not true?"

"Yes, Donnie." Now she was not calling him Don, but using a voice soft and whispery. "After you imagine this story, and see it as a possibility, you will be able to forgive yourself. So, who might have this authority over you? A bearded professor from your graduate days? A childhood buddy who was a con man at heart? Let's imagine a pretty woman. Give her hair color different than Valerie's or make her old like a wicked witch or your hated boss. Give her some characteristic that makes you do what she says. Maybe she's the head of some pirates or mastermind of a worldwide scheme. Got an image?"

"Sure, she's coming into my head at night, tying me up."

"Ok, so you have to do what she says, or else! Imagine how you would feel right now, how angry you would be. Even though you're not helpless, you need to do her bidding. Ok?"

"I can imagine being forced into this, maybe we won't get caught if I do as she says. I can imagine myself being smarter than her, like she's an evil witch making me hurt others. Or it's blackmail. I think I've got the movie in my head."

"Good work, Donnie. Let's imagine the rest of the story. Maybe the whole thing is beyond your control, and we know you like being in control. Soon you will feel some relief coming in, like a light in the darkness. Maybe you tried to escape on a boat. Maybe there's a storm. Or someone is chasing you. Maybe you get caught?"

"But I can't remember! All I know is that I nearly drowned." Donnie slumped further into the couch and turned his head into the pillow. He was giving up, as if he were no longer an adult. "You don't know how hard it is to be in this body and not know who I am. I'm locked up inside and I can't get out."

Dr. Cohen left her chair and knelt by Donnie's side. She soothed him as a lost child and said, "This is pretend, you can make the movie as exciting as you like. Pretend you stole something. If you admit this, even though you don't believe it happened, you will feel a weight off your shoulders. We will assume you broke your own code of honor system. All you need to do is forgive yourself. Tell me you're sorry like you mean it. You are very, very sorry."

Donnie imagined more scenes of his mental movie. Maybe he had cheated on the girl who loved him, or stolen something from her that broke her heart. His punishment was death by drowning. Killed her too? Got away from the cops but the sea wouldn't forgive him.

"I'm sorry!" Donnie yelled. "I'm truly sorry. It won't happen again." Donnie looked at the woman as she nodded her acceptance. Her face, at first stern, eased into a smile, almost motherly.

"How do you feel? Now that you are sorry for that thing you did, how long do you need to punish yourself? And Valerie? Has it been enough? Can you forgive yourself?"

Donnie looked up. "Oh, it's like penance. Maybe I don't need to know what I did wrong, but I am really sorry. My dad never spanked me; he'd have me do pushups. What should I do?"

Dr. Cohen smiled. "I'm not going to wash your mouth with soap, either. But tonight, when you get ready for bed, tell your wife how sorry you are for whatever you did before you met her. She will hold you, comfort you, and it will be enough. Her love will accept your apology, you don't have to tell her anything else. But in your mind, you must imagine your unknown crime and apologize completely."

Donnie could hardly believe this would work. Some weight had been lifted, but intellectually he knew the whole thing was a house of cards. He understood that emotionally he had to be sorry for something he must have done. If only his apology could be believed. But already he felt different somehow.

Donnie sat up feeling sheepish. The doctor's prescription had been like a trance, and intellectually he thought it was a bunch of hogwash. His critical mind had never allowed such emotions, such vulnerability. He looked up at Dr. Cohen who was back at her desk just waiting. He didn't know what to say.

"This is not hypnosis," the doctor explained. "It's improved guided imagery that follows certain parameters of your personality. As a child you strove for acceptance from a stern father, but your mother was more forgiving. I believe that if you fully imagine the scenes we concocted, and realize your small part in it, that you will find relief from some suppressed guilt. We may never know what happened realistically, but the pretend story should allow you room for forgiveness. Of yourself. I think you understand."

Donnie smiled. Reflecting on the doctor's words, he nodded. He had learned a lot about himself, and for the first time believed a psychiatrist had helped him. He felt light as a dandelion seed, the overhead fan almost lifted him from the couch. He felt like bowing to a master, but stood and extended his hand which she took with both of her own.

"Let me know how it goes with you." The doctor was smiling with conviction, and assurance that a breakthrough had been finally achieved. "We can have another session next week if you still can't forgive yourself. And if you find out what really happened, don't hesitate to come back."

As Donnie left the room, he moved the little box off the scarab. Symbolically, it seemed fitting. He waved goodbye to the doctor, left her inner office and walked through the waiting room. An elderly sad-looking woman sat waiting, along with another man who looked like an empty shell. Neither of them looked up. *I'm not like them anymore,* he thought. *I won't be back. I hope she can help them, too.*

12

Late that afternoon Val took the kids to fly kites out on the vacant prairie. For the third time she struggled to untangle Sadie's pink angel kite from Andrew's olive-green dragon kite string. Sadie's frustration began to boil. Donnie had taught the kids how to make kites early last year for such pastimes on hot summer days. Frustrated with the knot in Sadie's kite string, Val gave up, looked at the sky in frustration, and suddenly saw the face of her husband. Framed by the sunlight, his face glowed like an aura.

"Hi. . . Oh, Hi!" Val said when she saw his face in the golden light. "How did it go?" Donnie's face appeared relaxed and open like she'd never seen before. It was as if he'd won the lottery or found a treasure.

"I'm better, at least I feel a lot better," said Donnie. "Do you want some help?" He knelt down and took the tangled string from Val's hands. "Let's just cut it out" he said, as he took out his penknife to cut the strings and splice them perfectly back together. With both kites fixed, Sadie ran off with her pink kite which immediately took off in the prairie breeze.

"Thanks Daddy" she called as she ran down a little hill. Andrew mumbled a thank you while Donnie gazed affectionately at his wife.

"The doctor used something she called guided imagery on me. It's like voodoo magic but I feel different inside already. Actually, I can't wait to get to my desk and google some items Angus wanted me to search. He's been nagging me about some Irish myth stuff and some supposed connection with ancient Egypt. But I wanted to see you and the kids before getting lost in research. What do you say to going out for dinner in a while?"

"I'm up for eating out tonight. Suggestions?"

"How about Chinese? The kids like Chang's."

Valerie smiled and went to gather up their brood. Andrew had already snagged Sadie's kite again, so it seemed a good time for a reprimand and a curtailing of his spitefulness. Sadie had a mischievous grin on her face when Val pulled the kites down. Anyway, it had been a fun outing. The kids packed up the kites and ran ahead to the house.

Val grasped Donnie's hand as they walked behind the kids. "Gosh, you seem very relaxed and happy. Not like previous visits to a shrink. Did she give you meds while you were there?"

"I wouldn't take any stuff even if she'd offered. You know me better than that. Though I did like the incense wafting through her office. No, just some really vivid imagery while I reclined on a couch. Every time I tried to evade her instructions, she led me back into some story we concocted. Really weird. But at the end she had me apologize out loud, even had me yelling 'I'm sorry'. It felt like magic. Maybe that's why Catholics get a charge out of going to confession."

"Confession is good for the soul, or so they say," Val quipped. "Nothing wrong with catharsis. I'm relieved to see you so happy. Let's go get some Moo Shu pork."

A short drive brought them to Chang's Chinese. It had the usual buffet, gilded oriental furniture, but casual atmosphere for families. A large aquarium in the back held live lobsters waiting to be someone's dinner. "We're having an 'unbirthday' party," Donnie said as he looked at the waitress over the menu. Her Chinese face didn't register a question. "We'll have an order of pot-stickers, egg drop soup all around and some chicken eggrolls." She bowed slightly and wrote down the appetizers. Before she could rush off Donnie added,

"And a main dish of Moo Shu pork so the kids can fill their own pancakes. And something spicy, too. Kung Pao shrimp. Almond float for dessert with lychees?"

The waitress nodded, and hurried off with the order. "Today is my very merry 'unbirthday'" said Donnie. "I'm sixteen going on a hundred." Everyone laughed though Sadie had a quizzical look about those numbers. Donnie softly sang the song from the Disney "Alice in Wonderland" movie and then helped the kids practice holding chopsticks. They had more fun than they'd had in many months. After they finished eating, the waitress brought the check on a little tray with four fortune cookies.

"You will go to new places soon," said Sadie's. She was proud that she could read the words, and there were special magic numbers on the reverse.

"Be kind to others, always," read Andrew. He was quiet.

"Expect happy news from afar," said Val's. "That's easy, I expect to hear from Aunt Ali, and California is pretty far."

Donnie opened his last. He hesitated to read it out loud, but everyone had such expectant faces he had to deliver. "It says, 'You will find what was lost and return it'." His numbers were the usual string of lottery guesses, but included an unusual forty-two, an especially forbidden Chinese number. "It's wonderful how our fortunes fit." Donnie laughed.

But Sadie said, "I wanted a bunny."

Val reminded her, "We're going to Disneyland instead, and we'll get to see Aunt Ali And a trip to the tarpits, too."

Donnie smirked, imagining his kids running off the path and getting all sticky.

"Tarpits?" Andrew asked. "Is that in Disneyland too?"

"No, Disneyland is in Anaheim, and the tarpits are in the middle of Los Angeles. It's a huge city, lots of traffic, but they made a museum with fences around a natural area that oozes tar. It's called the La Brea Tarpits. 'Brea' is the Spanish word for tar. Like the stuff they fix streets with. Lots of prehistoric animals got caught in it, and there's a museum with their skeletons. Like mastodons and saber-toothed tigers. There's a kind of wolf and lots of birds, lots of vultures. The ancient animals got stuck in the tar, died there, and scavenger birds got stuck eating on their carcasses. Mom's right, we'll go there too."

"Is the tar stinky? And still sticky?" Andrew asked, letting his imagination run wild.

"You bet," said Donnie, "so stay on the walkways. I don't want to have to clean your shoes or have you fall in the tar. If you get stuck we might just leave you there."

Andrew knew his father was just teasing. He nodded and promised to not be rowdy, "I'll stay out of the tar. Maybe just poke it with a finger? I promise not to run around," he said, but his face had an impish grin. It was a promise almost impossible for him to keep. Everyone smiled, knowing that would be a first.

"And you can't run away from us when we're in Disneyland, either. It's a huge park with so many things to see, you could get lost. You don't want to make your mother worry now, do you?"

"Ok, Dad. I know. I want to see the pirate ride and Mickey Mouse. Can we stay there overnight?"

"No, too expensive. But if we stay past your bedtime, we'll see Tinkerbell fly from the castle, and fireworks. They have fireworks every night. We'll be there before you know it."

13

The stars were out when the family got back home. Val put the kids right to bed. They were too exhausted for a story that night, but the day had been perfect all around.

Val donned a nightgown and headed to the back porch. Donnie was already outside on the swing with two frosty beers.

"Come sit beside me, Sweetheart. The breeze is cool enough and it's a starry night." Donnie motioned with his right hand, drew an arc across the night sky. "The Perseids are up already if you look this way."

"They are incredibly far away, aren't they?" said Val as she savored a sip of the cool beer. "I guess that's good though. Earth still has no defense against a meteor strike. Everything would burn."

Donnie wanted to talk about something other than meteors. He missed intimate quiet talks with his wife. He deflected. "If you wished on a star, what would it be?"

"If you've really conquered your PTSD, then all we need is more money. I know you will take care of us . . . you will always be the wonderful man I married." She cuddled even closer to Donnie on the swing, their feet pushed in slow unison as if they were one person. Minutes passed as they sipped their beers. Then Val said, "Maybe you could write a book. I don't know what kind of money comes that way, but you have the 'creds'."

Donnie laughed quietly, thinking of subjects that might be worth pursuing. "Angus has been nudging me about some connections between ancient Egypt and our Celtic heritage. He keeps suggesting interactions between tribes of Sea Peoples and that period of time where all the major cities burned. As if fire rained down from the skies."

"Like a meteor strike?" suggested Val.

"Well, there's ample written evidence for a major asteroid strike in ancient days. Meteors and comets were observed by ancient astronomers, but thank goodness those celestial objects were just passing by Earth. But ancient records do tell of fields burning, months without sunlight due to smoke, and general misery that lasted for several seasons. Most of the major cities east of the Nile were demolished by fire. Like nearly everyone. Some researchers blame the Sea Peoples, but the cities were hundreds of miles from any water source. It's not likely that those berserkers would go so far inland. They were really just sailors."

"Is that the same time period as the Battle of Troy?" asked Val.

"Could be a factor. But Troy was attacked and burned so many times it's hard to correlate dates that might correspond to the destruction of other major cities. Research shows the major destruction happened in regnal year eight of Ramses III, at least according to written records across cultures. But there is no mention of Troy as a city. There are reports of a battle over a city called Wilusa in the Hittite kingdom, basically dated 1237 or thereabouts. It's linguistically easy to equate Wilusa with Illios or Illium. Hattusili III fought with Ahhiyawa and evidently won, but their kingdoms were destroyed over waring. Then the Egyptians took over. Am I boring you with this stuff?"

"Not at all," replied Val. "It's fun to watch you go professorial. Tell more."

"There is history about the Battle of Kadesh, which the pharaoh won, but that was mostly a fight against Hittites. No Greeks were involved. Even so, there would be no room for thousands of ships and fifty thousand warriors on that coastline. There's no harbor there, at least these days. Herodotus asked the Egyptians about it, but they had no records of such a battle. We assume the whole civilized area was under threat of either fire from the sky or looters taking advantage after some crisis. Then came a 'dark age' with no apparent progress in civilization for over four hundred years. Like they were just surviving rather than building cities and monuments All the shipping routes were lost, and cultures were just on their own."

"Is there any geological evidence of an asteroid strike?"

"Well, the Egyptians prized meteoritic glass in some jewelry, like the yellowish scarab in Tut's main pectoral necklace. They also scoured the sands for this kind of gemstone, and there are places in the desert where the sand is fused into glass. They also prized another type of glass called Fulgurite which is fused sand from a lightning strike. The only evidence of a meteor strike, besides tektites, would be geologic remains of a giant tsunami. If a meteor or asteroid even made a near miss across the area it might cause a tsunami. There is such evidence, thousands of miles away on Madagascar, where sea sand was deposited over thirty miles inland. It made something called 'chevrons', like triangular cliffs of this sand. The sand cliffs are full of sea creatures and stand nearly six hundred feet high. Only a huge atmospheric force could move that much sand so far from the ocean, or a huge asteroid. There really is no explanation for such cliffs of marine-sourced sand."

"So, no massive crater anywhere in the near east? Like the Gulf of Mexico?"

"Geologists are finding more evidence of what killed the dinosaurs, and think the Gulf was struck. The fossil fish in North Dakota have tektites in their gills from whatever hit in the Gulf. If something hit in the Mediterranean, the ocean is hiding the evidence. Geologists aren't much for reading the ancient histories like I do, but some ancient historians recall a time when that stretch of water was only a lake, not an inland sea as it is today. I can easily imagine such a catastrophe in the Mediterranean, where the tribes would resort to pillaging just to feed their people. I could make a case for the Danites, but not for some mythical Atlantis. If that tribe of Sea Peoples were the same as the Tuatha Dé Danann mentioned in Irish legends it might make a good read. People like coincidences like that. Maybe I *will* write a book, historical fiction stuff. Couldn't hoirt." Donnie began to chuckle as his mind thought of all sorts of connections. He could tie them together for such a story. "Would you be my editor?"

She poked him in the ribs. "Sounds like fun to work on it together."

"I think my nightmares are also ancient history," said Donnie abruptly. He put down his empty beer glass and embraced his wife. Then he led Val into the house to the bedroom, picked her up and tossed her gently onto the bed. It would be a glorious night and a new beginning to their happy life ahead.

Around three in the morning Donnie drifted into a new dream. It wasn't a nightmare anymore but a dream about sailors. *They were in an ancient galley, a triangular sail flapped against the single mast. It was nighttime, but not dark or moonlit. It was "in the gloaming," that eerie light in the Hebrides that is half-light but not dark. The sailors were screaming, arguing about their direction, and as they had no rudder, they steered only by plying the oars. The navigator was lashed to the prow, straining to steer through the width of the channel. In the semi-darkness, the steep cliffs glistened with the sea surge, waves lashed over the rail of their leather boat. The wind grasped at the men, pulled the hair off their shoulders and lashed at their eyes and cheeks like the whips of scorpions. Only the man at the prow could hope to see their path because the rowers grimaced from the sting on their faces. They knew their peril and dug their oars as if digging a grave.*

Shoulder muscles strained in pain, legs cramped, but at the last gasp of strength, the end of the channel came in sight. Suddenly, as if a door opened, at once the seas and wind calmed, and the sailors slacked their oars. Heads were bent in relief. With the roar of the sea gone, they heard women's voices singing in rhythm, chorus after chorus. The music seemed unending, forceful and rhythmic, as if it too could control the air. Sea birds from the cliffs swooped around the boat, diving and taunting at the exhausted sailors, even plucking at their wet linen serks. They had passed Corryvreckan, and the grasping goddess had been thwarted.

Again, the men took up their oars, and calmly rowed onward, confident in their leader to bring them to safe portage. The men joked, laughed at the sight of each man's hair, matted and tangled, even glued into spiky crowns by the salt spray.

"I would stop and taste the women here," called one.

Another chimed in, "the sight of you would drive them insane!"

"This is not our course, yelled their captain. It is not agreed. We sail on, another hour at most. Then you deserve rest before we meet the dawn. After three hours of rest, we will row home, and then find if your woman still recognizes you, my man! You should not waste your seed on that island."

The near mutiny avoided, the men bent to their oars and sailed on. They heard the women's voices for at least that last hour, until the breeze shifted and they came to a sandy deserted beach. Weary legs lifted their galley as they walked through surf to find rest. It was finally dark of night. With the boat beached, the men dropped to their knees and their well-deserved rest.

Near dawn, Donnie woke with a start. The dream seemed so real, with its fine detail, that he knew intimately how the men had felt. Sailing in far north seas must have been frightening in such dim light. But it could have been done safely, because island landmarks could have been lit by torchlight, as precursors of lighthouses which still dot the promontories of the Hebridean islands. Donnie thought the dream was odd however, that he dreamt of sailors instead of swimming. *I should be thankful for small favors!* Then he reached for the notepad and wrote down what he remembered of the dream. He was satisfied, replaced the pad and pencil, and tickled the slim waist of his sleeping wife. *This will be anew day in the corps!*

14

Early the next morning Val brought fresh coffee to the study and kissed Donnie as he sat in front of his laptop. He had a copy of Homer's *Odyssey* and a stack of photocopies from Medinet Habu. The ancient paintings of the battle showed some ships with bird-headed prows and warriors in horned helmets. Weapons included spears, arrows, slingshot, and fire. Some galleys were obviously Greek. Others Egyptian. So, who were the ones in plaid kilts and round shields?

Valerie put the coffee down, then stood by the doorway and watched Donnie's face relax into a wistful author's face. He seemed deep in thought, with closed eyes and an imaginative smile. It was a perfect sight of an author's reverie. He was trying to remember the dream about sailors, and was jotting down descriptions, never even noticed Val as she slipped away. She shut the door quietly, not wanting to break the spell she saw before her. The coffee would be cold, she would check on him later.

Donnie shuffled through papers until he found the depiction of monument walls at Medinet Habu. The ancient building was both a mortuary temple as well as a testament to the pharaoh's great deeds.

The battle scene could have been propaganda, but the artists seemed to be portraying reality. Different colors of paint had been applied to warriors' kilts, but skin colors seemed uniform. No one from Nubia, he thought. Donnie knew that Ramses III wrote about nine tribes of "Sea Peoples," each by name, all involved in the battles. Some were allies, some enemies. Warrior headdresses differed. Some wore plumed helmets, some had no helmets at all, but showed Greek beards and hairstyles. It must have been like a world war, with so many ethnicities involved. But there were no identifiable Persians in long flowing robes, which the Egyptians chided for looking like women. They held rectangular shields and spears. They weren't known as seafarers either. It was a battle at sea, but evidently Egyptians took prisoners, for later in the paintings, tallies of victims were recorded. Egyptians counted right hands and phalluses, for accurate counts. Pharaoh's tally of phalluses would identify which men were circumcised or not, and identify them culturally. If they had foreskins, they might be Celts. Heads were just a count of the slain. Those smaller parts would have been easy to count, then discard. Collecting or tallying heads happened only in other cultures.

Donnie sipped at the coffee, now barely tepid. He had lost track of time, and listened for sounds of the kids. Val must have put them in the backyard to play, as the house was quiet as a tomb. Images flowed through his mind as he began to write. Words came easily, perhaps because he planned a novel rather than some dry academic paper. His story would be set in Hyborea, a land beyond the north winds where the sun never sets. His seafarers would be Gaels, and it would be about the Battle of Troy.

15

Who Knows What Song the Sirens Sang?
1200 BCE

Iridescent moonlight illuminated the black schist beach, all else was wet with sea mist. The sailors marched single file, each carrying his hand-carved oar upright like a staff to drum on the impervious stone path until they reached the oracle cove. The drumbeat echoed off the sheer cliffs that surrounded their meeting place.

"*Leatha dhomh am Beinn a Cheathnaich, Air fal li oh, Oh lee Och Ooo!*" The galley song echoed from the rocks as they sang to the multitude of clans-folk awaiting their arrival. The single file of warriors curved around the slight rise until they were all assembled in the cleft of the sacred space. They halted in unison, dropped to one knee, and awaited midnight and the ceremony to come. With helmets removed, they bowed heads and listened to the waves break. They waited in solemn thought, breathing at each ninth wave, as the bonfire crackled and threw sparks high into the night sky. All watched in silence for the moon to start its descent.

A dark form attended the fire. This shrouded crone knelt by the fire to stir the basin of fresh blood, heated to near-boiling. The red viscous soup roiled and heaved as if still alive. Her rowan wand dipped, then swirled the blood until coagulated tendrils rose like the roots of some terrible spawn. Humming and cooing, she coaxed the red lines to rise into the dead still air. Pushing back the coarsely woven hood from her face, she let the tip of her wand trace an augury that only she could read. The lines of blood were tangled and spiked, interwoven until they formed a stinking, dense wreath that turned slowly like a cogwheel.

She watched the bloody wreath turn in the air, ever so slowly, then whispered an inaudible word. The tangled mass fell from the air. Blood splashed her wrinkled face, moonlight shone on her sightless eyes. She reached for her crutch and rose to speak with a slow gravely cadence that seemed consumed with the pain of her vision.

"Our world is not in balance," The sea itself seemed to quiet itself for all to hear. The sailors lifted their heads from meditation and stood silently, ready to receive the augury. "For generations we have known this. Though it is not of our doing, it is our warriors who are chosen to right this blasphemy that is causing the destruction of our homeland. Ice approaches to shorten our seasons, the seas lose their bounty, and salt-water rises into our grazing land. Our men must fight to bring back honor to the Goddess, and set to the torch all those who praise false gods. The time has come to bend the Earth to our Will, for we are chosen. Our people will prevail!"

The seeress, now flanked by other robed women, turned her blood-splashed face to hear their Queen's response, for their tribe was led by their warrior queen.

"Our warriors are most victorious. They have never failed. We see the task ahead, and have learned where they must sail," said Queen Maebh. "None can question their valor or strength. But to travel so far to right a wrong not of their doing? This is a high price. Do you see an-other path?" she asked of the seeress.

The crone's voice keened high into the darkening air. A cold wind rose in response, as if her report could even be questioned. The fire began to wane and sputter, even the embers went cold from the sea mist.

"How long since the sea began to encroach our best lands? Even good seaweed is absent for our cattle. We endure winds that once blew only farther south. Only I, as the eldest among us, remember days with-out darkness. Now nights grow longer with each passing season. Our world has shifted beneath our feet. These truths cannot be denied. Surely *some of our people remember a time of longer days and temperate winds. Those days are past, we must right the wrongs and return to balance. We, and only we, can lead all people back to the true worship." The crone's voice wove itself into the dark mist that hung in the air until all was still.*

Queen Maebh opened her arms to the heavens, bared her breasts, and accepted the oracle. She bowed to the priestess and her maidens convened there, and turned to her people who sat speechless on the hillside. Then she addressed the sailors who stood at attention to accept their orders. "Every season we trade further south. Our ships return with goods that are now necessities, no longer just desires. Soon, if the world is not righted, we must plan to leave our homeland forever. Which means warfare, taking new lands by force. Yet we have had peace beyond the north winds, far removed from those barbarians who have insulted the Earth. Are not mankind's laws given by the Goddess? We are not base animals, rutting out of season. Stealing a king's wife and throwing the world into war is not just a mistake, it is heresy of the highest magnitude. Sacrifices to false gods, made by men, have given us only disorder and grief. The honor of women and our Goddess will be restored. Only then will prosperity return."

The people began to murmur amongst themselves, but the sailors stamped their oars on the barren rocks until all would attend to their captain, Ullyxes. A giant of a man, he stood tallest of all the men, his chest rippled with muscles gained from work as the strongest archer the world had ever known. He spoke for his men in a loud, stern voice that rose above sounding waves: "Were someone to steal my wife, no miles or walls could keep me from vengeance! We have Right and Honor on our side. The Goddess Kirke will see us to victory. Let us prepare ships and armaments, arrows and slings of death. Sharpen your spears and axe heads, polish your helmets to shine in the sun. We will take the swift ocean course for speed, and plunder will make us golden when we return!"

Warrior sailors pounded their chests in agreement. Oars drummed again on the basalt beach, the cadence rose and fell like an assault on the foundation of their land. Raising his arm for silence again, Ullyxes continued: "Heaven is above us and earth is beneath us and the ocean is round about us. Unless the sky should fall with its showers of stars on the ground where we are camped, or unless the earth shall be rent by earthquakes, or unless the waves of the blue sea come upon the forests of the living world, we shall not give ground!"*

The oracle had promised success and the causes of the imbalance were made clear. The sailors had sailed many times to Troia and the surrounding bazaars of cities filled with blasphemous temples. This was not a voyage into the unknown. Families would be left safely behind, and would manage to live until the return of their warriors. As the crowds dispersed, each person accepted their various responsibilities for the coming war.

Cattle were slain as more skins would be needed to construct ships. Meat and fish, strung up on racks, were set to dry. Grains were baked for provisions, and whetstones turned to sharpen blades. Hard leather helmets were set with bull horns, bags were tanned for water, banners and sails were painted with the clan crests for all to admire. Wood was worked for more oars, drums and horns were laden in piles until nothing was undone. Each boat prow was carved into the shape of a seabird, for these boats would fly over the waves at speeds unmatched by any other force. Their flotilla of warriors would strike each city, until the true worship of the Goddess would prevail.

16

Pinelly and other mothers with wee boisterous babes had remained in homes to avoid disrupting the augury. She nursed her son, but he was fussy. Their spacious home of dry, stone walls was warmed by a central hearth. A cookpot of meaty stew simmered over the fire. The rectangular baby crib made of four vertical slabs of stone was thickly lined with animal furs from mainland hunts. The rising sun gave light filtered through the thatched roof as she cuddled the baby to comfort him. Here, Telly, go to sleep and stop your greeting. No more nipples for you to bite."

She snuggled her son into the furs and gave him his coral teether to suck on, since he had been working on new teeth. He now had a full belly, and adored his mother with satisfied eyes.

"I know your gums are sore. Bite this if you will, Sweet One, and if you draw blood it will be a taste of our bloodthirsty clan. Whatever comes will make you stronger."

The baby sucked his thumb-shaped coral and was soon quiet. Pinelly attended to her sore nipples with a bit of salted butter, then re-pinned her woolen sheath with her enameled penannular brooch. This was her finest treasure, given to her as a wedding present from Ullyxes. Her slender fingers traced the circlet as she hummed in the new morning light. Then she gave the stew a stir and awaited her warrior husband by lighting an oil lamp in the dark passageway that connected several homes of their clan. Before she could return to her loom, she heard Ullyxes singing his warrior song at the top of his voice. Telly began to wail in response.

"The Goddess smiles on us," he cheered, "for we will return with riches and booty, and fill our homes with gold." Ullyxes burst into the main room with the swagger befitting a drunken man, his face flushed with emotion. He threw down his heavy fur cape and sampled the stew with its wooden spoon. Then he sat, waiting to be served a meal, as if Pinelly knew all that had transpired.

Instead of serving him, she took up the baby and went into the next room. She unhooked her sheath at one shoulder and let Telly latch onto the nipple. Within minutes she had calmed the baby, then put him back into his furry crib. She stood with hands on hips to glare silently at her husband.

"Hektor and I are going to war! Isn't it terrific? We will plunder and fight, earn riches and glory, and come home victorious! We go to Troia to honor the omens. All has been foretold. Victory will be ours and balance restored. Be proud of your man, wife!"

"You do not need cheers from me, husband. I know you are the greatest archer, and the most superior warrior of all our people. You and Hektor can have an adventure sung in our history and put to the harp for all time, and I don't care! The danger and distance do not suffer you to think of us left behind. How long will you be gone?"

Taken aback by her scowl and harsh words. Ullyxes came down from the heights of his excitement. He rose, and with head bowed, embraced his devoted wife until she melted into his massive arms. His immensely strong chest enfolded her in safety until she forgot he would be going away.

"You are my pride, Pinelly. You will remain here in safety until I return. It is not for glory that sends us away to war, but duty to the Goddess and our way of life. I am the one who can fulfill the needs of our people. The Queen's orders will be obeyed, but victory is assured."

"How long?" again asked Pinelly?

"It might be more than a year to end this war in Troia, but with Hektor by my side, we will return safely. Before Telly even knows I am gone. You must respect my needs as a man of honor."

Tears filled Pinelly's eyes, soon her face was wet. She sought inner strength to not reveal the hurt she felt inside. She too was a warrior woman. If Telly were older, she too would be at her husband's side on the voyage. After all it was for the rights of women in the world, as well as the lure of plunder that the clan would fight. Unspoken words filled her face as their eyes met. Love strong as their great bed of a tree hardened against the world outside. Fleeting doubts quickly vanished as the sun's rays reached the floors. There was much work to do in preparation, and Pinelly would not refuse.

"What tasks are first for me to complete" she asked. "There is plenty of meal for cooking sea cakes. Bring the sacks from the storeroom while I milk the goats. Let Telly sleep, but when he wakes you can entertain him while I mix the dough. Let him bounce on your knee and tell him where you will travel. I cannot mix the cakes unless he is occupied."

Ullyxes quietly went to bring the sacks of meal from the next room. He was a giant of a man, and needed to bend low to enter the dark storage place. He came back quickly with two heavy linen sacks of meal under each arm. Telly sat up and laughed from his crib when he saw his father re-enter. After stacking the meal, Ullyxes scooped up his man-cub with one arm and took him to the seaside toilet area. Outside they played in the surf and sand. Telly's feet made footprints as his sire held his arms upright. He would be walking soon. Fleeting sadness crossed Ullyxes' face, realizing he would miss his son's first steps.

The two of them sat in the surf, Ullyxes with his son in his lap, and they caught the wavelets that danced into their hands. Burrowing snails appeared and disappeared, much to Telly's delight as Ullyxes told his son a tale of adventure ahead. His deep voice was calm as a stone cliff battered by useless waves. Telly enjoyed the warmth of his father's safe arms. With his son in clean linen, Ullyxes was proud, and hoped his son would understand his coming absence. It was all he could do.

17

As he paused and sat restively back in his chair, Donnie heard a tap at the door. Val popped in and said, "Lunch will be ready soon. How ya doin'? Maybe take a break?"

Donnie smiled, then offered Val the nearby chair so she could read over his shoulder. "My gosh, you've written almost two chapters?" Her face was beaming with pride.

"What do you think so far? Any questions or suggestions?" asked Donnie.

"Oh, I love that you have a spooky setting with a witchy seeress. Good start, and I can imagine the place where they were. It's an unusual title, though. What made you think of that?"

"I've long admired the questioning mind that was Sir Thomas Browne. He was a seventeenth century polymath, who speculated on all sorts of things you wouldn't expect, including the behaviors of Greek gods. He wrote a book about an urn burial, mostly full of aphorisms and he coined a lot of new words. He caused his contemporaries to question established truths. I guess it just sprang to mind from some antiquated statement he once made. Do you like it or should I call it the Battle of Troy, Revised?"

"No, I like it, just wondered where you got it. I like the descriptions of where the book starts, night but not dark. I remember being in Lewis in the 'gloaming.' The evening air is so different than anywhere else I've been. The lighting is like twilight, but it lasts for hours. Your story's place is even farther north?"

"The ancients believed 'Hyboria' means beyond the winds, and they thought it was so far north that it would be in daylight all the time. Maybe only a few hours of darkness. The ancient Greeks knew the Earth was a sphere, and thought if you were on the very top of the planet there would be no darkness, only continual daylight. You know at Summer Solstice Norwegians do some skiing north of the Arctic Circle. It's not called the Land of the Midnight Sun for nothing. I'm thinking of a place like Skara Brae."

"I saw some pictures of the ruins there once," said Val. "Some farmer was plowing and his machine broke into the roof of an ancient settlement. Before that, no one knew people had lived there at all."

"Yes, that's it. Over the centuries the village became covered by sea sand and peat, and the seas have risen a lot since people lived there. What land they once had was taken by the ocean. I read that there's evidence that for some reason they slaughtered four hundred head of cattle, had a feast, and simply left. I don't know about the accuracy of dating cattle bones being all slaughtered at one time, but the bones were arranged in a pattern that made it look that way. I can't imagine that much meat being processed in a short time. Why would they do that?"

"Maybe they were forced to leave? If they had to leave for some serious reason, like enormous flooding, they might not be able to take their cattle with them. Didn't they use cow leather for boats?"

"You're right! I can imagine a great exodus for some terrible reason, maybe even to escape enemies. If they suddenly saw the need to leave, like massive sea level rise, one thing they'd need is lots of boats. They could dry the meat, use the sinew for rope or for weaving the leather together, and turn the hides into leather for the necessary boats. I've never seen an estimate of the population that might have lived there, but the standing stone circle called Ring of Brodgar once had sixty stones. It would take an army of people to construct that. Many of the stones are twenty feet tall, like those at Stonehenge. I bet they were sorry to have to leave. Anyhow, experts claim they left all at once. Have you seen pictures of the settlements?"

"Yes," replied Val. "The homes and rooms look so cozy, interconnected with tunnels like the ruins I saw on Malta. You said Skara Brae homes were covered by thatch that fell in, so the contents were perfectly preserved. What artifacts were found?"

"That's part of the problem. The people must have had enough time to pack their belongings before they left. The houses were swept clean, the cupboards were bare. Because of a huge storm, the sand was washed away enough that archaeologists found the garbage midden, broken pottery and discarded stuff. But they took their tools and living articles with them There was no evidence of weaponry, seemed like just a peaceful agricultural settlement."

"The actual landscape must have been a lot like what we saw on Lewis, lots of wind and no trees?"

"Yeah, no trees or usable timber. Their boats were of hardened leather, bound with sinew. Most of their bounty just came from the sea. Lots of seafood, nutritious seaweed, and of course fish. The houses were built of stone, then covered with peat to protect them from the fierce winds. Inside must have been very cozy. Evidently, they grazed the cattle on what land they had, but fed them a kind of seaweed. I guess it must have worked for thousands of years until the sea level began to rise."

Val nodded in agreement. "Maybe add some more description of Ullyxes...I know he was the champion archer. Maybe give him red hair, too."

"Good idea," said Donnie, "I have to make sure he is identifiable as a Gael."

"And maybe make Penelope more angry? She's got a big part in Homer's story later on. Just a suggestion."

Donnie nodded in agreement. "I can't wait 'til the end of the *Odyssey* as I always thought of her being the hero of the story. She does her best to ward off the suitors. This is going to be fun."

"I'm glad to see you really appreciate my input," said Valerie. "Come for lunch, Sweetheart. You should take a break, maybe play with the kids. Andrew could use some instruction about how we'd like him to behave at Aunt Ali's. And at Disneyland. I want our vacation to be good times and not interrupted by disciplining him."

"Ok, of course. I know you were frustrated with his behavior flying kites. I don't ever remember being that competitive with my sister, but she is older than me, of course. Family constellation and all that. I'll see what I can do about a little more structure for when we're in California. Sorry to have been so busy with research and stuff. And the writing is pretty interesting for me. I guess it takes my mind off all the mundane problems we have."

"Like what?"

"Like the house is too small, like money. Like my job at the department. I try to ignore stuff 'cause I don't know how to fix it. I'm excited to write a novel, but maybe it's just a diversion from real stuff in front of me."

"I love you, you silly guy. I'm not worried. Let's go have lunch, and you'll feel more inspired if you play with the kids for a while. I'll get the laundry done." Val gave Donnie a little shove on the shoulder and skittered off to get lunch served. This was not the time to add any more stress, and she liked the idea of Donnie writing a novel.

18

California weather was doing its best to retain its residents in spite of the high cost of living. The sun shone brightly in the clear blue sky as if the land didn't understand that other parts of the world had seasons. Ali was tidying up her kitchen when Angus phoned to check on what time Donnie and the family would be coming. Seeing his name on her caller I.D., she picked up immediately. She was anxious to talk to him before the family would be at her apartment, even her ragged fingernails evidenced the tension she felt about the visit.

"Thank goodness you've called tonight. I've been wrestling with how to handle our problem. I mean even the first thing to say. We can't screw this up."

"Aye," responded Angus. "Been thinkin' o' oor plan. Do ye agree 'tis best to hold off on giving Donnie the papyrus until just before they leave? That way we might not be spoilin' their whole visit."

"Good idea," replied Ali. "I'm expecting them in three days. I've been mostly cleaning and straightening up the apartment. But I took the papyrus home and found a safe place to hide it before the big reveal."

"I'd like to give him the translation first, see what impression it makes. I've been asking him to research the name of Scota but he hasn't found anything except for what's on Wikipedia."

"What's on the internet?"

"Just that the legend says Scotland is named for a queen of the Scotti . . . they called her Scotach. This is the mythical Celtic warrior queen who 'lowers her shield' each Halloween night to permit the departed souls to visit from the Otherworld. That's the Celtic New Year's Eve you know."

"Halloween? Guess they had a different calendar for New Year's," said Ali, "I didn't know that. Well, I agree we should first show him his own translation of the papyrus and go from there. Let the kids be off playing or sound asleep, but have Valerie sitting with him, of course. She's a good support."

"Aye, we're on the same page," said Angus. "I've got some Disneyland passes to get to you for them. Should save a bit o' green. I'll drop them off tomorrow to your mailbox, and then wait for you to invite me over when it's best. Oh, and I'll bring along a good single malt. We might all need more than a wee nip. Thanks, Ali, See you soon, bye."

Angus hung up the phone and played the scene over and over in his mind, as he fiddled with his wee dram of Scotch. Behind closed eyelids his eyes darted to and fro, like some caged bird with torn wings. The legend of Scota had concerned him, all his life really. When Ali first showed him the papyrus at his office, his shock at seeing evidence for the Egyptian princess nearly knocked him out of his chair. He remembered immediately locking his office door, something he never did especially when there was a young, attractive female 'Co-ed type' visiting alone. Angus knew he could easily be a target of rumors, being that he was the only unmarried faculty member in his department. And his office, being in the basement, didn't get a lot of visits. University scandals wouldn't help any careers, and the rather dapper Scot had plenty of female admirers. He remembered that day as if it were yesterday, and now their efforts had come full circle. The delay had been necessary, but Angus believed it had been long enough.

Now they were about to disclose the mystery. Revealing it to Donnie seemed the best plan to let them all go forward into resolving the mysterious papyrus. And Angus wanted the truth to be known more than anything else in the world. Messing with Egyptian pharaonic chronology was one thing, but proving the Celtic migration would be quite another.

The main indisputable fact stood that they knew the papyrus was mailed from an island near Gibraltar. The wrappings on the parcel of bath salts had been discarded, but both Ali and her old roommate had seen the address. So had Angus. They also knew the papyrus wasn't a fake, or just a souvenir from some gift shop, Angus could attest to that. Everything about it, the musty smell, its color, its ink, even its glyphs, rang true to its authenticity. Angus tried to imagine the scene.

Maybe Donnie would remember what he did if he actually held it in his hand? Maybe he would even say he stole it? Then again, he might even deny the handwriting was his, or accuse me of forgery? Would he tear it up in anger, knowing he'd been caught pilfering an artifact?

Angus thought of the many traps in chess an opponent would be compelled to move, against no hope of avoiding check. It was a real-life zugzwang with no way out for any of them. His mind was caught in a continuous loop of various outcomes. But he couldn't imagine a happy moment of what Donnie might do when they presented the papyrus. Would he cry out in anguish or slump into a ball?

With only pieces of the truth, and medical records, Donnie could probably negotiate with the Academy of Archaeologists and not be in danger of renunciation. It would be totally unfair to jeopardize the young family man's credentials. But since when is the world fair? Angus might force the gamble for personal reasons of supporting the myth as authentic, but Ali thought it would help Donnie in the end.

Angus was prepared to testify to what he knew, and hoped that would be enough to square with the academics. He would make sure Donnie had Ali's copies of the amnesia report, and that all would go well enough to prove that Donnie didn't know how the papyrus came into his possession in the first place. Unless of course Donnie had intended to be unethical. Angus poured another nip of his favorite Dalwhinnie, which ironically translates as "meeting place." The amber liquid soothed his throat. He left a lot of his anxiety in the empty glass, but not all of it. Tonight would not be the first sleepless night of many he'd experienced since the whole affair took place.

1 9

"Spit spot!" called Valerie to the kids playing with toys in their bedroom. She often used references to Mary Poppins when she wanted quick action from the kids. "We're packing today. The plane will take us to Aunt Ali on Thursday. We'll take clothes, but we have room for only one toy, and pick one without a lot of pieces that might get lost while you're sitting on the plane. And Andrew, no remote cars."

"Daddy and I will pack one big suitcase too. The weather will be sunny and warm, so maybe some shorts? And your swimsuit. Aunt Ali has a pool at her apartment. If we have time after we get there in the afternoon, you can go swimming." The kids' excitement had swelled into happy cheers. "And, don't bother Daddy in his study. You know he is working on a new manuscript. Just get moving!"

"Oh boy, we're really going." Sadie clapped her hands and pranced around the room with her little pink suitcase. Then she put it on her bed and began trying to fit toy after toy into it first. At least her swimsuit was an easy fit.

"One toy!" ordered Andrew. He was really too grown up for taking along a teddy bear, so he looked around before selecting his favorite T-shirt that had pirates on the back. He knew boardgames were not a choice, but he did have a new book of mazes. He decided that and a pencil would be ok for a while.

After a few minutes Valerie came to check on their progress. "It'll be a whole weekend, plus a day at the tar pits, so pack at least five underpants. See what all will fit. We can always buy more clothes in L.A., but I want to see how you can plan ahead." Val cocked an eye at what Sadie had packed, and laughed. "Sadie, only your most favorite bear."

Then she went to check on Donnie. Pausing at the doorway Val heard Donnie's fingers tapping over the keys. Sunlight streamed through the room, but the laptop itself illuminated his face with a beatific glow. "Try to get to a stopping point?" she suggested through the open door. Her soft voice might have caused Donnie to pause, but she doubted that he'd heard her. She then decided to quietly come into the room.

Donnie sat silently, not noticing that Val was nearby. He was lost in thought, totally oblivious of his wife's presence. He imagined the words before his fingers typed them but he seemed to have stopped in mid-sentence.

"Writer's fugue?" she asked as she planted a kiss on his forehead. "I've got the kids packing. Did you forget we leave tomorrow?"

"Nope, I'm just having too much fun. I think this story is working. . . At least I know the tribe's escapades on their way home. The goddess 'Kirke' seems synonymous with 'Circe' including shape shifting and transforming humans into animals. Irish legends are full of people being turned into cows, swans, or other things, even more things than the Greeks. Our seafarers will get caught in a whirlpool, which could have been the one called Corryvreckan, off the coast of Barra, by the north tip of Jura. You know, that island near Mull. Inner Hebrides."

Val nodded as if she knew those things, but her face was quizzical. "You act like we went there on the trip to Lewis, but I don't remember the names of those islands. But seems like there's Celtic legends about sacrificing the queen's consort to a whirlpool?"

"Oh right." Donnie smiled and beamed in pride as he turned to Val. "I'd almost forgotten about those Celtic practices the Romans talked about. According to Plutarch, there was an island called

Ogygia five days' sail from Britain. Funny that they knew it was a 'five-day sail.' He wrote that's where the daughter of Atlas kept sacrificial consorts. This is also called the 'Sacred Marriage' or *hieras ganos*. This daughter of Atlas was known as 'Atlantis' and the cemetery on the island has lots of burials of so-called 'princes' from lands far away. Like Denmark."

"Sounds like a continuous orgy," Val chuckled. "Would some handsome specimen of a man really choose sex for ten years knowing he was doomed to sacrificial death in a whirlpool?" She looked at Donnie, expecting to hear him say he'd do it if it were her. But he didn't take the opening.

"Well if they believed in reincarnation strongly enough, maybe they'd volunteer. Legends say women didn't cut their hair during the seven years, then donated long braids of hair for a special rope. After attaching the braided rope to a huge millstone, men would row out at low tide to secure the rope deeply. Then the rope would be attached to the coracle for the ride into the whirlpool. The little round boat would be forced to travel in circles, at increasing speeds until the sacrificial man was thrown to his death. In Homer's story, that goddess is a nymph named Circe, but she sure mimics the Celtic goddess named Kirke."

"Homer gives Ulysses even more problems, because he fathers a son by the goddess or nymph named Calypso. Later when Ulysses comes back, this son actually kills his father. Then Telemachus comes for revenge. I guess Ulysses has to go back to Calypso when Telemachus doesn't recognize him or something. Heroes would do anything for love!" Donnie stroked his thighs in an enticing way as he laughed. "Wanna read this new chapter?"

Valerie smirked, thinking of all the preparations left to do. "I'll read it right now but I still have more packing to do before we go. And I want to make sure the kitchen is clean. I hate to come home to a messy kitchen. Go in the kitchen and have a sandwich before you burn out." She took the papers from Donnie and sat in the recliner to read.

The dark sea menaced; waves lashed the shore. Ullyxes had been obedient to the priestess, actually enjoyed her bed for these many years. But his heart longed for home and the family that he hoped kept his memory alive. Calypso found him brooding by the sea, as whenever he left her palace and had drunk his fill of wine, he sought solitude on the rocky beach. Counting the waves crash, he did not hear her come behind him. Her petal soft hands stroked his shoulders, enticing him back to the grove. Then she spoke: "After all these years with me, you still desire your old home? There is only adversity ahead. How can this be more desirable than I?" But Ullyxes did not answer. She continued to get his attention. "The years of your pledge are nearly done, I know, and you have fulfilled each day admirably. Yet, the coracle awaits, and Corryvreckan will form at the next full moon. Would you give up your mortality or live in beauty with me?"

"Oh my Lady, am I given the choice? My sweet Pinelly would seem a shade before your majesty, death and old age being unknown to you. But still I am heartsick each end of day. If the Goddess wills it so, I will brave the whirlpool and meet the bare rocks at the bottom of the sea."

"If you do not return to me, our son will be orphaned, unforgiving. No other consorts have returned to me, but you are the strongest, mightiest warrior to have ever landed here. I think you could survive the test. My love for you is not the judge, only your strength of arm and desire. You have kept your pledge. Our time was well spent."

She smiled that enticing smile so well known to her consorts. "I do release you to your choice. But know this: If you do survive the whirlpool, there will be no other ship waiting to carry you home. The coracle will be fitted with but one oar, one oar to guide you down and down. I will weep to see you go, but I will not wait for your return."

Ullyxes stood upright on the rocks, then knelt before the nymph. Gazing up, he lifted his chin to her shining face, and Calypso could see that his decision was made.

"Give me but one wineskin of water, and my tartan cloak. The sea will bear me out with the tide, and I will wait for the voice of Kirke. My life will be in Her hands and in my own strength of oar. Until then dear Lady, leave me. Alone I must be. I would look homeward."

Donnie waited for Val to finish, as he thought that chapter had reached a good ending point. He sat pensively, wondering what to write next. He didn't want to rewrite the entire *Odyssey*, only the parts showing the voyage home after the main battle.

Val looked up after reading the excerpt and said, "No misspelled words that I can see. But I thought whirlpools were just random currents. Does it happen because of rocks in the ocean?"

"Well, sorta," said Donnie. "Evidently there is some tall volcanic spire deep underwater near Barra that causes an almost continuous whirlpool. Some accounts say it happens three times each day. It's impassable with certain tides, or storms, and the locals invented all sorts of myths to explain it. Like it's the watery tunnel to the underworld. If the whirlpool was used for sacrificing the goddess' consort after seven years of service, I hope they treated him like a king before they threw him to the waves!"

"Do you really think they sacrificed people like that?" asked Val. "Maybe that's just another Roman exaggeration about how savage and barbaric the Celts were. I find it hard to believe human sacrifice was ever widespread."

"Well, you know we have valid evidence of human sacrifice in many ancient cultures. In Peru people sacrificed their children to the sun god. In Mexico they cut living hearts out of sacrificial captives. In Irish stories there's the Wicker Man, and there's that Norse practice of sending a maiden off in flames on a funeral barge. I guess I'd believe it, after all, we're talking three or four thousand years ago. The ancient burial grounds on the Isle of Barra have records of those who were sacrificed. Some prince from Denmark, named Brechan is supposed to be the origin of the name Corryvreckan."

Val nodded, and her eyes began to tear up thinking that ancient people could believe life was more meaningful in death than in living. She wanted the best for her kids, and couldn't imagine giving up a child, or for that matter, a fearless warrior, to be sacrificed.

"Even believing in reincarnation, that would be hard." Val sat, thinking out loud. "I do remember Romans, like Julius Caesar, making fun of the Celts because he said they'd take out a loan, with only the promise to pay it back in the next life."

Then Donnie hugged Val and said, "Yeah, I've heard that one. People can believe all kinds of magic or religion, and act out of intense belief. If reincarnation is real, get ready for me, 'cause I'll choose you all over again." Then he kissed Val with passionate kisses, as if they were teenagers again. "But, back to work!"

Donnie released his wife and left her sitting there. He wanted to get another solid chapter written about the Trojan Horse. Who knew how much time he'd have to devote to this book idea? *Strike while the iron is hot,* he thought.

2 O

The galleys, upturned on the rocky beach, lay some distance from the main attack point. In this haphazard arrangement, the boats appeared abandoned. Ullyxes and his most trusted captains huddled under one overturned hull. It did little to shield them against a cold wind that seemed unwilling to desist in punishing the frigid men. A pitifully small fire of driftwood glowed, struggled to warm meager leftover fish stew in a clay pot. Darkness fell around them and the men could not see other's faces. Sand fleas pinched at uncovered flesh. Their wet woolen cloaks smelled of home far away.

"So that's the plan, men," whispered Ullyxes. "At moonrise we'll take our gift over to the main gate. Push it quietly even closer. Then the chosen men will board. It will be deadly cold inside. Weapons must be wrapped against any noise. Our other ships must look disabled. Our main force must stay hidden until the gate opens. It will be a hard, final run on the rocky shore, maybe too long for cold legs, but we've no shelter to hide behind on this cursed bloody beach. They must believe we've gone, with just the gift of the horse and a few wrecked boats."

Ullyxes paused, waited for others to either show their support or rebuttal. Only grunts of approval came from the men. Then they dispersed, gathered up their clansmen to hide themselves farther off the rocky shoreline. Under cover of darkness, the city lookouts had but little chance to see where the invaders hid in the blackness of night. It would be a long night in the cold, with no warmth of fire or heated food. The men would wrap themselves in their woolen plaids, which would keep their bodies from freezing, but at the battle's charge their kilts would not their cover their cold legs. Men would huddle together, arms at the ready, for the final onslaught to come.

Ullyxes ran his right hand over the smooth side of their construction. Staves of broken galleys formed the back of a giant wooden horse. Another boat formed its belly. Just before midnight, before moonrise, twelve of their strongest warriors would crawl inside. The boat sides, with seaweed ropes lashed in such a tight pattern, assured that no boards could give way. The bird head prow, now altered by their artisans, was fashioned into a great horse's head with a gaping mouth. Torn flags formed a mane and tail which flapped wildly in the night breeze. Dozens of huge round shields formed wheels, able to roll on the flat basalt, assuming the Troians thought to pull it with the braided rope. The heavy pierced stone that had sufficed as anchor lay ahead of the false horse, as an invitation to pull it inside the city gates. If they chose not to pull it, the gates would at least be open for the onslaught. All was in readiness.

Ullyxes sat next to Hektor as they waited for midnight. Head heavy with regret, the battle-scarred hands held fast at his temples. His eyes watered, but not from the cold wind. Wet tears shone on his cheeks.

"My liege, what saddens you so?" asked Hektor. "Do you doubt our victory? Those are our strongest warriors, and they will not fail." Then Hektor whispered, "Or did you want to be with them?"

Ullyxes coughed, shook his head. "No, my friend, I am deeply saddened by our plan. There is no honor in it. Shame lies heavy on my heart that this plan was chosen. I believe that it will work, and that the city will soon be in our hands. But a feigned surrender for entrance through the gates does not sit well with me. Better I would die, unarmed in battle, one-on-one with their king."

Hektor clapped Ullyxes on the shoulder. He had none of those feelings in his heart. "It still will be a hard fight. If the sun does not shed warmth on our warriors, and their bodies be too cold or their swords too dull to cut the lashings, we will certainly be in for a hand-to-hand fight. We fight for our Goddess Kirke, to right the world, by whatever

114

means we can devise." He paused, then offered, "Perhaps the Bard can sing of this battle in glorious words. Words that will turn your heart with praise. We will return home with a glorious, victorious report."

Ullyxes spat soured phlegm. "So be it! We will return home with magnificent spoils, and the world will revere us for our victory! Let them say what they will, our warfare will not be forgotten."

Donnie wrote those last words, then went to the kitchen for lunch. His family would journey to sunny California tomorrow, rest that evening, and then spend a day in the happiest place on Earth. *I'll leave that latest chapter out for Val to see but right now I'm hungry!*

Donnie went to the kitchen where Val had arranged a variety of fixings for sandwiches. He handed his writing efforts to Val, then sat to eat. Val read through the description of the Trojan Horse victory rather quickly. She had practical matters to attend to, and didn't give it her full attention. At least it was a short excerpt and had no glowing mistakes in spelling.

"Well, that answers my questions about making the Trojan horse. I sure do like it so far." Then she left him to resume packing. It would be good to get outta Dodge, and the kids were so excited they were causing a ruckus in the bedroom. Val kissed Donnie on the cheek and then went to attend their kids.

Donnie intended to write a longer version of the siege of Troy when they came back home. He thought his descriptions of the night before the battle were close to how he imagined that night; it must have been very cold. After that he planned to add a chapter about the warriors Nestor and Hector. Donnie chuckled to himself thinking about how often those Greek names occurred in Scottish history. Scottish parents chose them for their sons as often as Calum, Tom, or Ian.

As Donnie sat eating his sandwich, he also knew he would write more about the interaction between Ulysses and Calypso. If the legends had some further depth, and historical meaning, that goddess or nymph was the feisty daughter of Atlas himself. She had been banished to an island, and spent her days luring princes to her bed. They came as consorts for seven years in most legends, only to meet a watery death. Ulysses became her consort, but he had lost his men on a different island where Kirke had turned them into pigs. If Ulysses was a Pict from Barra he would have known about 'Glenn nac Muc,' the Bay of Pigs. And Scylla's Cave which is clearly described by Homer as a cave with two entrances. It is just east of Corryvrechan, and supposedly had six-headed monsters inside that didn't allow passage to the other side. On Barra another cave, referred to as MacCrimmon's cave, was a place where criminals were executed. If they were able to get through to the other opening, people would forgive their crimes. According to Homer, Odysseus stored his sailing equipment in a large cave, whose description matched perfectly.

But what if the men had instead wanted to stay on Kirke's island? Having found a good place to live, perhaps they mutinied and decided to join the people there, instead of travelling into unknown waters with Ulysses. With so many islands in proximity, each seafaring family became a clan. Each clan had its own war cry, motto, and crest design. There are several modern clans that boasted a boar on their crest, so that joining with the clan, perhaps getting it tattooed on one's chest, would be synonymous for "becoming a pig."

Donnie went back and forth between his copy of the *Odyssey* and other ways of reading between the lines. If the seafarers had needed new boats in order to get home, they could have found the necessary skins by slaying the "cattle of Helios." What if the slaying of the cattle was the slaughtering of the herds on Skara Brae? Homer calls the island "Scheria" which isn't too different from the "bay of Skaill." It takes an extended amount of time to harden the leather into suitable boat skins, according to the Brendan Voyage, but the ships could easily hold twenty or more men. Perhaps they had to leave Skara Brae due to climate change or other problem. Their lovely homes had certainly been deserted on purpose. According to

Homer, Ulysses' boat was made of hardened 'oxhide and wood' that he was able to lash together to escape Charybdis.

Donnie thought the story about Polyphemus, the one-eyed giant, or troll, might be easy enough to imagine. . . Giants or no giants, there are plenty of huge caves in the Hebrides, and on the mainland. Goat and sheepherding would have been common. Besides, only parts of the *Odyssey* need be explained in Donnie's novel. All of these could be explained as having happened in the North Atlantic. Those people were the great seafarers of their time.

But there was another factual tangent bothering Donnie. The relatively new DNA research into human genome sequencing included investigation into the rhesus factor that occurs in human blood lines. All people, except for an odd forty-three rare people called 'Goldens,' have either Rh-negative or Rh-positive blood. According to geneticists, all human beings originated in sub-Saharan Africa many millions of years ago, but the Rhesus factor happened only around twenty million years ago. Somehow, Rh-negative humans must have been isolated perhaps because they had already left the African area. It was as if they lived on some island that had no contact with other humans, whether Cro-Magnon, Denisovans, Neanderthals, or any other human sub-groups. Wherever they lived, there must have been no cats, neither big or small, domestic or wild, because Rh-negative people have no genetic antigens for the parasite that causes toxoplasmosis.

Donnie had long been interested in a particular subset of human evolutionary line called 'Haplogroup X'. This DNA group predominates among Berbers, Basques, Canary Islanders, a clan of Scots-Irish, and some 'Black Irish.' Donnie had long considered them 'his people' as both he and Valerie were Rh-negative. Perhaps it was why they were so compatible. There were other strains of the Haplogroup as well. It included northern Native American tribes, such as the Ojibwa, but also the Navajo. Most curiously, the trait surfaces in the Ainu of Japan. These populations retained the

Rh-negative blood line, ostensibly because intermarriage with other Rh-positive people had adverse effects. Blood incompatibility could not be ameliorated as it can be nowadays. And if the DNA could be proven to have a central source, as from an island, it would explain this dispersion if their homeland fell because of some cataclysm. Geologically speaking, this must have happened over twenty thousand years ago.

According to Plato's dialogs in the Critias and Timaeus, the island of Atlantis once existed west and 'beyond the Pillars of Hercules.' This fabled land of prosperous people had wealth in rare minerals and metals. Hesiod even calls them the 'Golden People.' According to the legends they produced a form of a copper and gold alloy called 'orichalcum' which was reputed to cover the whole temple to Poseidon. This made it shine in the sunlight, and the 'laws of Poseidon' were supposedly inscribed on the walls with this metal sheathing. According to Plato, the island sank over ten thousand years earlier. This was not to be confused with the more local destruction of the Minoans or Myceneans. The legend lives on, as artifacts may still be found. A shipwreck discovered off the coast of Sicily in 2015 was found to have carried a cargo of this ancient metal. In 2017, divers recovered forty-seven ingots of orichalcum and another 39 lumps of the reddish metal. The ship had sunk 2600 years ago.

Although the dialogue with Critias is incomplete, another odd notion about the fabled Atlantis is curious. Plato mentions that the shepherds liked working there because they earned "thrice their normal pay." Somehow Plato knew that the nights were sixteen hours long. They must have joked about it, and evidently believed it must have been very far north. Donnie found it interesting that the ancient Greeks knew about the unusual workday length in those northernmost islands. Even in northern Scotland summers have light until eleven in the evening, with daybreak around three in the morning. Of course, this is reversed in winters.

Since this only happens farther north, as the ancient Greeks named it Hyboria, that is 'beyond the winds.' Plato recounts in the Timaeus that the island continent was destroyed by a gigantic flood which caused the island to break up and sink beneath the waves. If those islanders escaped in boats, they would be dispersed from their island to the nearest landfall. This would of course be the islands of the Inner and Outer Hebrides, the Canary Islands, and eventually the western shores of Spain and northern Africa.

Could the Arctic have melted so quickly that there was passage over the pole? Or could the water levels risen so deeply that a northwest passage to Japan would be possible? If so, that would explain why the Ainu of Japan also belong to Haplogroup X. Perhaps the end of the last Ice Age was more catastrophic than geologists believe, and there was a biblical worldwide flood. Donnie stored this idea in the back of his mind. He really wanted to write at least one more chapter before they would leave for California. But his lineage drove him to know more about this branch of people, and their history. He was immersed in thought as he chewed his sandwich.

Val had other things on her mind. Her intention was to use up whatever food was in the fridge that was perishable, because they would be gone four days. Uneaten bread would go into the freezer and the vegetable bin held just a few carrots and a head of lettuce that would stay fresh. She was planning a hearty soup for dinner, again so there would be no leftovers. Since they were planning to leave L.A. early on Monday morning, grab some lunch at the airport, Monday evening would be just a quick stop for fried chicken on their way home. *Men don't think of these things,* she thought, *but I like being in charge of this household. Every penny we can save will help against the cost of this vacation. I'm really a person who likes organization, 'cause then I don't feel so uncertain when things get exciting.* She was back, bustling around the kitchen, furiously straightening things on the counters and just taking a mental inventory of stuff on hand. Her activity level sometimes made Donnie irritated, as it imposed on his train of thought.

"Want a coke with that?" Val asked as she came nearer, cleaning up dishes. Donnie was eating the last few potato chips, mostly crumbs in the bag. Val took the near empty bag from his hands. "You don't need to eat those crumbs," she said.

"Yeah, sure. I'm glad the kids didn't wait for me. I know I took longer than you expected."

"No problem, I sent them to straighten up their room and finish packing. They are really excited about going to Disneyland, and the weather reports look like sunny days ahead. Andrew is really hyper, but Sadie is doing better to contain the craziness."

"That's good," Donnie replied. "Going to the park on a Friday should have fewer crowds than on a Saturday, which should shorten our waits in line. It's been a long, long, time since I went to California, I know my parents took me there only once. I still have good memories of it though. Our kids will too if we don't have to yell at them."

After Donnie had used up all the leftover lunchmeat and finished his sandwich, Val cleared away other stuff off the table and sat down.

"How's it going? Did you finish the chapter about the Trojan Horse?"

"I think so. It's hard to imagine the character motivations, but I think it's right. After that I wrote a chapter about the battles with Hector and Achilles. I guess later I can rearrange the chapters so they get in the right order. I re-read the stuff Homer wrote about Calypso, and she seemed like just a self-centered tease. Homer's gist about the Trojan horse seemed to imply that Ulysses was not very proud of himself for the trickery. I read somewhere that researchers thought maybe the horse had plague victims or some sort of pestilence inside that would kill the Trojans, and that it wasn't full of soldiers after all. My view of Ulysses shows some shame, but not downright treachery like germ warfare. Got any opinion?"

Val thought a bit, shook her head. The mundane tasks of running the house, getting packed, and planning for the big trip were all she wanted to think about. "Yeah, I don't think our sailors would resort to something that repugnant. But I guess they didn't have rules of warfare, just their own code of honor. I'm glad you thought about it though, it makes the story more interesting. When the hero does something morally wrong, he's no longer heroic."

"I'll give it a rest until we get back," Donnie said. "Maybe take the kids out to play some ball outside, get them tired enough to sleep well tonight. It would even be good if they fell asleep on the plane. Wish we could get four seats together."

"No chance of that, but maybe we can switch you and me or separate the kids? I have packed some books for them to read on the flight, and they really like it when you read to them."

"What did you pick out?" asked Donnie.

"Actually, I thought they might like *Treasure Island*. Have you done that with them yet?"

"Nope, good choice though. Andrew loves stories about pirates. I thought it was so interesting that Stevenson befriended a young man who suffered from tuberculosis of the bone. He would bodily carry his friend to a coach for fresh air and take him on outings. The patient hadn't heard the sound of running water for years. The man eventually had a leg amputated, which was the basis for Long John Silver. I'm just a newbie as an author, but I can see how the regular happenings in a life can be woven into a story. It's easy for me to understand the predicament of Ulysses, as I certainly couldn't leave you and the kids for ten years."

"No, you're not allowed. I couldn't take it either. One of my sorority sister's husband is going to prison for absconding with some company funds. They have two kids. I don't know how she's going to handle it. Get a job, I guess."

"I wonder if writing this book will really help us out enough. We should be saving money for college funds, and of course emergencies. I hate to see you working for pennies at the museum, but keep looking for some other opportunities. OK?"

Val nodded. "I could find something like teaching assistant at Sadie's school, though. Might pay a little more, and the schedule would be perfect. I've got an application turned in already."

Donnie got up, embraced his wife and kissed her on the ear. "You're the greatest! Love you so much!" Then he went to get the bat and ball and collect the kids.

21

After a quick breakfast of cereal and blueberry muffins, Val and Donnie packed their kids into the car for the short trip to the Central Illinois Airport. They parked the car in the extended trip lot, as it was cheaper to park their car than take a taxi to and from the airport. Checking in was a snap, the lines were short, and they had only a short wait at the terminal.

Sadie and Andrew stood at the window and watched planes taxi to their loading docks. In the distance they could see other planes taking off on a runway while other planes were landing. It was a busy airport, though no comparison to O'Hare in Chicago, but it gave the kids a taste of what was to come on their trip to California. Learn to wait, patiently.

Then the attendant announced it was time for boarding, and any passengers with children or the elderly were called to enter the plane before the rest of the group. Their suitcase wheels made a rumbling sound as they walked toward the door of the plane. Andrew was in a hurry, as always, but hesitated when he saw the little gap between the gangway and the plane door. Donnie smiled when the stewardess welcomed them in and said she'd see them later.

"Go find a good seat," she said.

The first open seats were just behind the cockpit doors, and the bulwark gave extra legroom. Sadie went first and sat by the window seat, but they had already decided to take turns watching out the window during the flight.

With carry-on luggage stowed, Val sat beside Andrew and Sadie, and showed them how to adjust the seat belt. Donnie sat at the window seat directly behind them, that way he could talk to the kids between the seats.

"You'll hear the sound of the engines soon, and feel the thrust of their power. It's a lot stronger than anything you'll feel in a ride at Disneyland, but here we go!"

After the stewardess gave the emergency instructions, the plane was ready to take off. Both kids felt the pressure on their bodies as they felt the surge of the jet engines, but they were smiling and unafraid. After they were in the air, the stewardess came to visit with them. From her pocket she took out two plastic pins, emblazoned with the airline's name and spread-out wings. "Now you are honorary pilots" she said, as she pinned a pin on each chest. The kids were thrilled and thanked her for the attention.

"Now the hard part," said Donnie. "This flight takes over five hours, and there's a layover in New Mexico. You can spend time with your maze and activity books for a while. There won't be anything to see out of the window except clouds." Val retrieved pencils from her purse, stowed under the seat, and the kids got busy. But pretty soon they were bored, and those things were put away. Val and Donnie changed seats, and Donnie sat between the kids so he could read to them. He had brought a large-print paperback copy of *Treasure Island*.

Donnie read a few chapters, with occasional pauses to discuss what was happening in the novel. There were some lessons to be told about 'black spots' and trusting adults, and what it might have been like in eighteenth century Scotland: children being necessary and able to work, the British class system, and the Pirate Code were all discussed. Vocabulary words such as being marooned, ship terms such as fore, aft, astern, Union Jack, and many others came up in discussions. After another hour or so had passed, Donnie had hoped the kids would nap, as Valerie was already sleeping behind them.

As soon as Donnie paused in his storytelling, the stewardess came by with her rolling cart. Soft drinks and peanuts were offered, and though no real food would be served, the kids were happy for the interruptions. Before they even finished their sodas, the captain announced they were on time to land at the Albuquerque International Airport.

The plane took a distinct turn as one wing dipped toward the earth, and the plane made its flight path over the Sandia Mountain Range. Andrew leaned over Sadie and they both watched the flight zoom over buildings and streets below. Then they felt the wheels bounce down on the runway, in an almost smooth, uneventful landing. They waited patiently for instructions before leaving the plane, gathered all their luggage, and walked out excitedly to see what lay ahead.

The Albuquerque airport, in its colorful effort to welcome guests, had a mariachi band playing outside a Mexican restaurant. There were display cases with Native American artifacts, weaving, pottery, and a lot of jewelry. The layover allowed time for lunch, so they promptly got seats in the first restaurant. It was like a foreign country, none of the items on the menu were things the family had ever seen before. The waitress suggested tacos for the children, with a spicy sauce called "salsa" on the side. Val ordered a combination plate of enchilada, relleno, and a tamale, just to experience the different foods. Donnie ordered empanadas and a bowl of posole. Chips and salsa were on the table to sample as well. The food came quickly, along with a basket of fried bread that looked like little pillows.

"These are 'sopapillas'," the waitress explained. "Bite off one corner, then drizzle in some honey while you turn it slowly around. That's a sweet treat for you." Then she bounded off to the beat of the mariachi music.

"This is a 'fiesta'!" said Val. "A real introduction to Southwest culture. Lots of Native American spices and flavors mixed with the Spanish culture from Mexico. You can each have a bite of what's on my plate, too, it's not too spicy." But the kids both thought it had more than enough spice for their liking, good thing they only took the tiniest samples. "We have enough time to enjoy a rest here, but we'll keep an ear out for announcements for the next leg of our trip." After they finished eating, there was time for an excursion around the building.

On one wall was a display of flights/departures and various destinations. Donnie checked and verified their next terminal destination. Also on the display were local time and weather reports. The outside temperature in Albuquerque was 98 degrees, but the humidity was only twelve percent. "That's drier than the Sahara," said Donnie.

"This is a high desert plateau." said a nearby lady. "Once the humidity registered at zero, but that should be impossible. If you need to go out, take water with you." She smiled and went on her way, happy to be home.

The family wandered through various shops, saw lots of tourist trinkets. Everywhere were t-shirts with the New Mexico yellow flag and Zia Indian symbol. Other shops had replicas of dinosaurs, as New Mexico had once been the migration path for prehistoric animals. *Maybe someday we can have a vacation in this area,* thought Donnie. *It seems rich with all kinds of history.* Then the announcement came that their flight to Los Angeles would be boarding soon. A moving walkway took them to another terminal, and the Cameron family was off to California.

The next plane, crowded with people, appeared at first to be too full of passengers to allow the family to sit together. The same stewardess took initiative however, and asked a few passengers to switch seats so that the kids weren't separated from a parent. It would be a very short flight to LAX, and everyone seem happy to help the Camerons.

Andrew sat at the window seat, and watched the clouds fly by. Then he exclaimed, "Dad, I see the ocean!" Sure enough, their plane was flying over ocean water below, making its turn to enter the flight path for landing. Again passengers felt the roar of engines as the pilot slowed the plane for the approach. Everyone cheered when they felt the wheels lightly touch the asphalt. Flying across thousands of miles was certainly an improvement since the time of the wagon trains.

Following arrows, the family found the baggage retrieval carousel. Sadie and Andrew watched for their smaller suitcases, which came down first of all the bags. Donnie retrieved Sadie's pink case and set it at her feet. As he did so, a voice behind him said, "Welcome to LA, brother mine!" It was Alison, on time to pick them up and take them to her home.

"Aunt Ali!" yelled the kids in unison, "we're here!" Hugs and kisses all around while they waited for the larger suitcase to arrive. They were in luck, for nothing was lost, and a quick trip through the airport took them to Ali's car.

"I thought it might be nice, if you're all not too tired, to take a short trip to the beach?" she asked. "It's sorta on the way home anyway."

Everyone cheered at that suggestion, and though the traffic was scary and clogged as usual, Ali took them to Long Beach to see the ocean. Val told the kids they could take off their sandals, and only wade in the water, to not go all the way in or get very wet.

"Watch the waves as they come closer. I don't want to take wet kids in the car," said Ali.

The children obeyed, dug little holes in the sand with their toes, and experienced what it was like to walk along a beachfront. Little shellfish were easily uncovered in the sand as each wave rolled away. Sadie collected some seashells, nothing very large, but some were colorful. The kids had never seen the ocean before, and thinking back on their story of pirates, Andrew had a wistful look in his eyes. Seeing the expanse of water for the first time was striking, and of course he wanted to go on a boat ride.

"Can we go on a boat ride, Aunt Ali?" asked Andrew.

"Sorry, not today. But maybe you'll all come again for a longer stay, and we'll do that. Today I just wanted you to see the ocean and feel the sand in your toes. Let's get back to the car. You guys can go swimming at my house."

"Really? I can't wait," said Sadie.

On the drive to Ali's apartment, she explained to everyone that the apartment complex had a pool for residents, and they were welcome to use it. "I'm the manager of a Yoga Studio. So at least I had time and could pick you all up at the airport. Tomorrow you're going to Disneyland, but I have to work. So, it's your job to tell me all about it. Promise?"

"We promise," said the kids in unison. Donnie, relieved that he didn't have to drive in this congested traffic, sat back and enjoyed the California weather. Val was happy that the trip had been so uneventful and smooth. Her kids had behaved well on the plane trip, and they weren't the least bit cranky. So far, their plans were working well.

After another hour in the car Ali pulled into her apartment complex. Donnie quickly carried in the suitcases, opened them and the kids got their swimsuits out. Val said she'd take them for a swim and let Donnie have some time with his sister alone. So off they went into the California sun with an assortment of towels.

"What's new out your way?" asked Ali. "I don't hear enough of you these days. Guess you've been busy?"

"Yeah, although it's summer break, I'm inundated with research from Angus. He has sent so much paperwork and cross-references to validate, that it hasn't been much of a vacation from the office. But I guess that's what we professors like to do. I haven't spent as much time with the kids as I'd like, so tomorrow will hopefully make up for it. Can you take the day off on Saturday and go to the tar pits with us?"

"Sure, I'll take you there. Sorry I can't go with to Disneyland, but gotta earn my money. The rent is so high out here, if it wasn't for the weather, I'd be gone. The yoga studio is doing well though, keeps me busy, and I like it."

"Any serious boyfriends on the horizon?" Donnie asked. "Any chance I can vet them like you used to do my ladies?"

"Nope. Haven't met anyone worth my time," replied Ali. "Sorry if you thought I was too critical of those girls you dated. Remember that one named Kemi that I hated? She was scary."

"No, don't remember her. Why was she scary?"

"She was just kinda domineering, seemed like she could get you to do what she wanted. I think she's the reason you went to Spain in the first place. I just got bad vibes from her."

Donnie nodded, but turned the conversation into talking about the kids, and their lives so far. Wanting a dog, school starting up, and Val looking for a position to earn extra money. It was a nice afternoon with his sister, something he hadn't had for a very long time.

"You know I was sort of a behavior problem in Kindergarten," said Donnie. "Since you're younger than me, you might not have realized that. We see some of the same hyper behavior with Andrew. I guess you've noticed he likes to run all the time."

"He seems alright to me," Ali replied, "just a boisterous little boy like any other."

"Well, going to a new grade and a new teacher is always a challenge for him. Good thing Sadie is calmer and will be happy to be in an all-day class. Anyhow, we're hoping this trip to Disneyland and you will be enough to occupy his brain awhile, and let his feet rest."

"Gotcha. It'll be great. They'll want to hit the sack early tonight no doubt. Do you think they will sleep ok on the couch sectional?"

"Yeah, or on the floor. I might stay up pretty late myself though. I'm still having night terrors once in a while, but I'm lots better. I'll even sleep with the kids if I need to, or put Sadie with Val. We'll play it by ear."

"Okay, I won't worry about it at all. It's just great to have you visit with me. Sorry my apartment is so small, but I couldn't afford a three-bedroom place. Mostly I wanted a pool. So, the one spare bedroom seemed to be more affordable. But you wouldn't believe what it costs to live out here. I'm paying nearly 2K a month, at least utilities are included."

"Wow!" Donnie exclaimed. "My house rental is only half that. Guess I should be happy with what we've got. But Val wants a bigger house, and the kids deserve to have a bedroom each. We're thinking of moving. I want to write a book on the side for more money. But my co-workers at the department are really stodgy. I get the cold shoulder sometimes."

"There's lots of opportunities for someone with your credentials. I think you've settled down more, now that you have kids. But what happened to the soldier of fortune you used to be? I never thought you'd be some quiet professor. Surely, having kids hasn't tamed that wild streak coming from our red hair?"

Donnie laughed and shook his head. Ali knew him pretty well, and he saw the same dynamic with his sister that he saw with his own kids. Sadie being a girl, seemed more mature than Andrew, at least she also stood up for him like Ali had him. He was happy to have this afternoon with Ali, and they sat and relived old times until the kids came back with Val.

After dinner, everyone went to bed early. The airplane trip had taken more out of their energy than they had realized, and tomorrow would be a very exciting day.

Even though the Camerons arrived early, the long line for entrance moved so slowly the kids could hardly stand it. Raring to go, it was all Donnie could do to get the map unfolded and decide which kingdom to head for first. Val had supplied each child with pennies in their right pocket, with instructions to seek out as many of the coin-squashing machines they could. Those flattened pennies would make memorable souvenirs at some later date.

First they headed to Fantasy Land, as memories of the book about Alice were still in their minds. Sadie explored Rabbit's House with glee, and after they had taken a ride on the Tweedle Dum snail they were ready for the Mad Hatter's tea cup ride. This spinning cup could go faster if Donnie turned the wheel, but it was a big mistake to show Andrew how to do it. The kids could hardly wait to go on another ride, but at least they found Donnie's weakness right away. No more spinning rides, or their father would just stand and watch.

As it was still early in the day, Val wanted to avoid most of the gift shops they passed, as she didn't want to be encumbered with too many items to carry through the park. One interesting attraction was called Animation Academy which gave participants simple drawing instruction. Both Andrew and Sadie learned to draw Mickey Mouse cartoon figures as the instructions were step by step. Val thought that skill might come in handy some day, just learning to draw noses entertained both kids for a while.

Donnie headed his family toward Critter Country where they met all the characters in the Briar Patch. Of course, neither of the children had ever seen the movie "Song of the South" as the Disney corporation had censored it from the American public due to its portrayal of racial culture in the American South. Donnie put Uncle Remus Stories on his mental book list, as he thought everybody should understand the "reverse psychology" Brer Rabbit used to avoid being caught. They still had fun there listening to the wonderful songs and seeing the characters' antics.

Around lunchtime the family boarded boats and went on a jungle cruise to view the realistic animals along the banks of the jungle river. Sadie laughed at the baboons, though the crocodiles were scary. She knew there was nothing to really harm her, even though they all did get a little wet. They learned that if the animals were real, the hippopotamus held the most danger in travelling down a river in Africa. At the sandwich shop there, after eating, Andrew smashed a penny in the machine outside and got a leopard imprint, even followed directions to keep it separate by putting the coin in his left pocket for safety.

The sights and sounds were overwhelming! Sadie couldn't have been happier when they took a ride through the One Hundred Acre Forest, as she knew all the songs. Donnie did a good impersonation of Tigger, and hopped right into the Disney Dress Shop nearby. Val had promised Sadie she could have a princess dress for use at Halloween, so the girls spent time looking at dresses with lots of pink netting and sparkles.

Donnie and Andrew sat outside while they waited for Sadie and her mother. "Do you like any of the characters in *Winnie the Pooh*?"

"I like the idea of how the toys were all friends," said Andrew. "And the bear gets so fat and stuck in the tree from eating honey. Would bears really attack a beehive?"

"Most probably would," said Donnie. "Evidently their fur is so thick they don't get stung except on their noses."

"Well, I guess I like the Owl best. He seems pretty smart."

"I think the author wanted to have different personalities in his story. He made Kanga very motherly and Eeyore very sad. I thought you would say you liked Tigger the best, since he is always hopping around so fast. You're doing a good job at staying with us today, and I'm proud of how you've been patient. Look at the map. You can choose our next stop."

Andrew looked at the unfolded map and immediately stabbed his finger at Pirates of the Caribbean ride. Donnie guessed that would be Andrew's next choice. "Done!" he said. "Great choice."

Just then the girls came out of the shop. Sadie couldn't have smiled more broadly, as she had her special dress in a nice tight package. Val pretended to wipe sweat of her forehead.

"It was a hard choice to make, but we did it!" she called.

"We're off to see pirates," said Andrew. "I hope it's scary."

The boat cruise through the pirate's lair did have some scary scenes, but Sadie knew it was just for fun. They learned the pirate song written by Stevenson so long ago, "Yo, Ho and a bottle of rum." Val said that the low-level lighting made the trip more realistic than the brightly lit African cruise had been. Anyhow it was fun and both kids squashed coins as the family left that attraction. They headed now to Big Thunder Railroad, for a ride on a roller-coaster train. Donnie looked at the map when they got seated in the train car, to make sure they didn't miss something on their list. The train ride was exciting as it went through huge dinosaur ribs, past skulls, and all sorts of mining paraphernalia.

Val checked her wristwatch and motioned to Donnie. They only had a few hours left to see so much more of the park. They knew they couldn't do much more in one day, but there were several more attractions to see before they went to Cinderella's Castle. The family passed by the Haunted House, mainly because the lines there were so long. At least there were signs at various places that told how long the wait would be for each place in line. That was a big help, for sure.

They walked to Splash Mountain. The sign said riders had to be forty inches or taller to ride. Sadie got measured, happy to know she had grown to forty-four inches already. "I'm a big girl now," she stated, so they got to go on that rollercoaster ride too. An automatic camera took a photo of the family just as they splashed down. In its cardboard frame, that would be another memorable thing put on the wall when they got home.

The last thing the family did before heading out to the castle was to visit Chip 'n Dale's Treehouse. Of all the Disney attractions, this monstrous tree with its small doors and colorful railings proved to be the ultimate favorite of kids everywhere. It was more popular than shaking hands with Mickey Mouse or Princess Belle. The child-sized stairway through the tree limbs prohibited the bigger adults from entering, but Val was able to accompany the children easily while Donnie took pictures. He got great shots of them leaning out of various windows. He knew he was in trouble almost immediately when he saw the ecstasy on their faces.

"Dad, Dad, can you build this at home?" called Andrew. "You promised a tree house, remember?"

Donnie waved, but knew their biggest tree at home couldn't support such a construction. Still, with a lot of imagination, and maybe some struts for extra support, he would give it his best shot. He knew the fun of having an off the ground hideaway would be a wonderful asset to that little rental house on the prairie.

There was one attraction geared mostly for adults that they came to next. This was a shop full of assorted treasures, antiques, and objects of interest to adults. Most of the items were extremely pricey. Shelves of Egyptian reproductions, scarabs and ushabtis were available, as well as Polynesian tikis and assorted swords. Andrew really wanted a sturdy plastic pirate cutlass and pirate hat, so that went into the shopping bag. It was not life size, so Val assumed it would fit in the suitcase for the trip home. Donnie marveled at the assorted scarab reproductions, selected one like the one in Dr. Cohen's office.

He thought he'd make himself a cloud-covered box for it too. Val sized up the t-shirts, purchased one each for her and Donnie, and two each for the kids in two sizes. She expected Andrew to want to wear his pirate shirt 'til it wore out and expected Sadie to want to sleep in her Cinderella pink.

As it was getting late, the family headed to the main castle for Peter Pan's Flight ride. The spinning contraption wasn't for Donnie again, but he held a place in line while Val took the kids to the candy shop. They had to find some coconut candy for Ali, and maybe some cinnamon bears for later. Pretty soon they joined Donnie in the line, gave him all the parcels to hold and took flight with Peter. "I can fly!" was the song, and Donnie remembered as a small boy he once jumped off the roof with a sheet, thinking he could fly. The movie actually had to include a warning for parents, to explain to children that you need pixie dust to fly. It takes more than a bedsheet, and some children had gotten hurt thinking that just believing strongly would allow them to fly. Still it was a nice memory for Donnie as he watched his family circle overhead.

Twilight was falling, shadows lengthened, and many of the attendees were heading to the main gates, and the trip home. The Camerons however, found a small restaurant for their extended purpose, and found good things to eat. It wasn't too expensive, though Donnie's credit card had quite a large new balance to pay off when they got home. Soon it was dark enough for the fireworks show, they paid their bill and found a good place to sit outside to watch the show.

"I wish we could live in California. We could come here all the time," said Sadie.

"I'd move in with Aunt Ali," said Andrew. "I like sleeping on the floor, it's like camping out." Both kids looked wistfully at their parents.

"California is a really expensive place to live" said Val. "We probably could afford a little apartment like Aunt Ali, but Daddy would have to give up being a professor. There are hardly any teaching openings out here, since lots of people want to live out here, too."

"I wouldn't mind moving," said Donnie suddenly. "But you kids have no idea of the hurdles I had to do just to teach at Bloomington. I'm not a very famous archeologist, and they only hire the most famous teachers."

"What about Mr. Morrison?" asked Andrew. "Is he really famous?"

"Fame is not what I meant, so much," said Donnie. "It's a matter of how much he's published, researched, and contributed to his field. He has a long list of accomplishments."

"But he's old," said Sadie. "He has a grey beard and talks funny. I don't want my daddy to look like that."

Val and Donnie chuckled. But thinking of moving wasn't such a far-fetched idea for either of them. Val often repressed words when she found Donnie complaining about the department, as it was her mission to support Donnie with whatever he wanted to do. But it was obvious to her that a change of scenery would do them all some good. That house is just too small. And she was usually the adventurous one in the group.

The crowd oohed and awed with the first burst of fireworks. Silver and blue bursts glittered the night sky. A spotlight illuminated a brave lady dressed as Tinkerbell as she flew from the castle turret. She carried a wand laced with sparklers as she made her descent to the castle roof. The crowd cheered; more fireworks sparked in the sky. Disney knew how to put on a great show, and it had been worth every smashed penny and credit charge, the memories would live forever. Donnie thought this experience would stand like a fortress against anything bad that could happen in the future.

2 3

"Hi, how was it? What did you think?" Ali asked when the family of four burst into her apartment late that night. They'd waited until dark so the kids could watch Tinker Bell fly from the castle through the fireworks. But it was late, and the ride to the apartment hadn't cooled their enthusiasm.

"I want to live here!" said Sadie. "We could go every day and still not get to do all the rides." She twirled around the room with her magic wand and the pink fairy dress they'd found in one of the gift shops. Getting her out of it for bed would be the next challenge.

"My favorite was the Pirates of the Caribbean," said Andrew. "We went on a jungle boat and saw alligators and snakes. And Daddy got all wet on the ride down Magic Mountain." Then the boy plopped on the floor, completely exhausted. With his big smile showing a missing front tooth he could have passed for any scraggly toothed pirate. Then he took out all his smashed pennies to look at his cache. He and Sadie tried to put them in order on the rug.

"Having a plan before we went really helped," said Val. "I could bring drinks to the kids while Donnie waited in line with them and stuff like that. No one seemed to complain when we rejoined the lines. But I don't think we did fifty rides. Maybe forty-nine."

"I could have skipped the Tea Cup ride," said Donnie, "guess I'm not good at spinning rides. I got pretty urpy. Give me a roller coaster instead. It was extra good having those coupons from Angus. We didn't spend as much as I expected, and we were able to treat the kids to a great time. They'll never forget this trip, and neither will

I." Donnie looked wistfully at his sister, and gestured with his arms in thanking her for the hospitality. "We could never have afforded it without your help. It's our treat tomorrow though."

"Let's get the kids down, they must be super tired," said Ali as she led them to their pads on the floor. "Tomorrow's another day, and I'm going with. Come along you two." She ushered the kids to the bathroom to brush their teeth. They got pajamas while Donnie and Val went to the kitchen to raid the fridge. "Thanks so much for this wonderful vacation," called Val as she looked for something to drink. She smiled so lovingly that her face just beamed. The day had gone without a hitch, the kids behaved like troopers, and there had been none of the issues she expected. Telling them that the line was too long at the Haunted Mansion worked too. She didn't want the kids to have scary dreams, or be frightened later on. Good thing Donnie was on board with that decision. At the park they had watched other parents struggle with belligerent children, but both Andrew and Sadie enjoyed every minute of the park. There was one near-issue, as Andrew wanted a rubber pirate cutlass. Ordinarily Val would have nixed that, but with promises that he'd never swing it at anyone, or tease Sadie with it, he got his wish. And it could fit in the big suitcase for the trip home.

Val carried two glasses of lemonade to the table. "Want something stronger?"

"Nope, this is fine," replied Donnie. "I'm just thirsty, and can't wait for bed. I'm so proud of how our kids behaved today. Guess they're not spoiled like some we saw today, begging for everything."

"We don't need to leave early tomorrow for La Brea, do we? Sleeping in would be great."

Donnie smiled in agreement. "Nope, and weekday traffic shouldn't be much of a problem. Ali can drive us after a good breakfast. I'll kiss the kids goodnight, see you in a minute."

Valerie cleared away the lemonade glasses and went to the guest bedroom, slipped off her clothes and went soundly to sleep as soon as her head hit the pillow. It had been a glorious day. Worth whatever coin they'd spent. The photos of all the rides and things they'd seen would carry them through hot days back in Illinois. She felt a sort of completion inside, as if old worries about Donnie being a good husband and father were now gone. The Disneyland trip was like the honeymoon they never had, and Val smiled as she fell asleep.

Val was lightly snoring when Donnie crawled into bed by her side. The apartment was quiet and he thought about how lucky he'd been with his life so far. His parents could never afford such a great vacation; in fact he couldn't remember much of his childhood beyond story time with his dad at night. Nothing special stood out, really. His parents never did anything out of the ordinary, and never expected much of him. Now with his position at the university, two great kids, and things going our way, Donnie felt complete, but it was only momentary. *Val has supported me though all those night terrors, and she's been so great.* The book he planned might bring in some extra money, and things were on track.

For money! *Those Sea Peoples!* thought Donnie. *How could they support their families by pirating when they were gone so long? The clan system would support mothers and children of course. But was this usual behavior, sailing long distances for booty? According to Homer, they were gone ten or twenty years, and Telemachus was already grown when Ulysses got back. Going all the way to Ilium must have been an uncommon route for them so they probably wouldn't expect to be back in six months. We know they traded in tin from the Thames area, as it was not found in the Mediterranean. But the tin mines in Cornwall had been played out. There was a crisis for making bronze, so a good reason to pillage. Of the nine Sea Peoples named by Ramses III some could be identified as coming from Sardinia, but the descriptions at Medinet Habu showed warriors that looked like Celts. The round shields were one thing, the horned helmets were another. Plaid kilts? The Irish annals called them Tuatha Dé Danann, or tribe of Dan. So maybe they were really mercenaries from Judea? Or were they really Gaels all the way from the Isles?*

Donnie thought about the route from the Hebrides to Egypt. *By staying within sight of shorelines, they could probably make the journey in a month or two, fight at Troy, and then head on home. But the siege of Troy took a long time according to Homer, and even if the battle scenes were just put in for excitement, the time away from home would have been hard to deal with. I couldn't be away from my kids for any length of time,* thought Donnie. *I'd just die.*

The part about being turned into pigs was another issue. They could have joined Clan Campbell, and gotten tattoos of pigs for their initiation. Maybe the men felt they would never get to their home island, and that that was the best alternative, to make a life with a new clan. Makes sense, muttered Donnie. *Hadn't Ulysses warned his men about not killing the cattle? Then Helios refused to bring back the sunlight?*

As Donnie lay there musing, he thought he heard the whistle of a train, far away. *Life isn't linear,* he thought. *We'd like to believe things just go on ahead, step by step. But those ancient mariners probably didn't concern themselves with the future. They all believed in reincarnation, or at least a trip to the Otherworld. Just like going through a door, no worries about death. Wish I could live like that. Well, we'll take one day at a time, and see where life leads. Tomorrow it'll be making sure Andrew stays out of the tar.* Somewhere in the back of his mind Donnie was imagining a bend in the road. Like things were too good. Like winning an award he didn't deserve.

He listened to his wife softly breathing, and snuggled closer to her warmth. What could he do to guard their future? He doubted book sales would be significant, and though he could publish future articles with Angus' help, the academic life wasn't enough to send two kids through college these days. *I got over my night terrors, but can't even afford a better house so Andrew could have a dog.* Donnie began to feel inadequate, though he had accepted the park passes with gratitude. And having Ali put them up was another blow to his male ego. *Think you're pretty smart? Yeah, we'll see.*

2 4

The Page Museum at the La Brea Tar Pits in Hancock Park (once just a fence around some dangerous ground oozing sticky tar) has a wonderful exhibit of Late Miocene and early Pliocene life on Earth. Years of excavation and research had yielded the remains of many prehistoric animals, animals now extinct. Severe climactic changes around twenty thousand years ago during the Pleistocene marked the end of almost all large animal species on the North American continent. It had been a period of extreme warming, which evidently changed migration patterns as well as habitats. Large mammals and many other species could not adapt and became extinct.

With excavation of these tar pits, paleontologists had a virtual linear record of climactic change. Scientists scoured through these fossils in order to close the many punctuated gaps in the fossil record. Currently a huge expansion of the museum was underway, in an effort to provide much needed underground parking. Expanding the parking lot would have been impossible due to the astronomical costs of land in the Los Angeles area. The excavation unearthed a deluge of new fossils, some never before seen in the fossil record.

This new excavation was called Project 23, because researchers now had an additional twenty-three huge boxes of new fossils to categorize. Evidently a newly identified small cat had once existed along with their huge Sabre Tooth cousins. A little larger than the modern house cat, this animal had never been found elsewhere on the American continent, though small cats were ubiquitous on all other continents on earth. The presence of this cat had enormous ramifications in understanding even the evolution of Homo Sapiens and human blood types which geneticists were researching. Donnie had brought his family to the museum, not realizing at the time how these new fossils would augment his mind-set of human evolution.

Ali had not visited the museum since she was a child either, and was startled by the expansive remodeling that was underway. The perennial problem of parking in Los Angeles mandated the construction of a new parking lot to enhance the museum for tourists. After managing to avoid all the construction, Ali found a parking spot, and they excitedly walked to the doors. Soon the family arrived at the main entrance, where the children were met with models of giant mastodons. Long ago their enormously heavy tusks proved inadequate for getting out of the deathly mire. Sadie craned her neck and saw the animal tower above her. Andrew stood there with his mouth wide open in amazement. The kids were actually speechless, trying to imagine what it would have been like for a person to become prey.

"I'm glad they're gone," said Andrew. "I thought the ride through the fake rib bones yesterday was too much make believe. But these guys were really that big!"

As they entered the display area, the family saw models of animals in lifelike positions. Most of them appeared to be preying on others, and then they got trapped in the tar themselves. Dire wolves, vultures and saber-toothed cats were caught, with many other species of animals from bugs to birds. But it was the behavior of these varieties of species which led to whether or not they became extinct. The average person would have believed that the fiercest animals would have had better survival, but the tar pit discoveries showed the opposite.

Coyotes, which were found in large numbers, were pack animals, using group tactics to attack large prey. Watching a member succumb to the tar evidently taught the rest of the pack to avoid the danger. The ancient coyote survived to the present day because they were small, scavenger types, who worked together. Large predators such as sabre-tooth tigers hunted alone, and did not have such a warning. Giant bears, and mastodons, because of their bulk, could not extricate themselves from the sticky tar. Dire wolves which hunted smaller prey or were lured by the sounds of struggling animals, also fell victim to the deep tar.

Of the three and a half million fossils found, over six hundred species of animals were preserved. Many specimens filled the evolutionary gaps, since the tar pits had been trapping animals for thousands of years. Evidently humans visiting the place in ancient times knew better than to approach, for no bodies of humans had been preserved there.

The kids stayed by the adults as they walked through the museum, occasionally Donnie would read a plaque, but lots of technical explanation had the kids tuning out. Although it was cool inside, there wasn't enough of what you might call "interactive" for kids, though there were exhibits demonstrating how scientists painstakingly removed the fossilized mud from the bones. Cleaning and categorizing the bones was a methodical and slow process, one that Donnie valued highly. He liked doing that sort of digging and reconstruction, for he had the patience needed, absent in most people. He could have happily stood there for hours, or taken up a digging tool, but the kids were getting antsy.

Exhibits compared the lengths of teeth, and showed the difference between the skull of a coyote and a wolf. The tooth of the sabre tooth cat was the especially long and curved, and the comparisons were interesting to the adults more than the kids. After an hour or so of walking around, the family decided to go view what was outside.

In the bright sunshine, the museum had a wonderful garden exhibit of bronze statues, showing the dying anguish of those trapped animals. Val wasn't sure her kids were old enough to view the faces of death, but Donnie wanted to give them a lesson in natural history. To him it was part of nature, though cruel, and he wanted the children to be exposed to the scientific view of things. They had spent more than an hour inside, so it was good to go out and actually see the actual tarry ground. Dozens of sculptures circled around the pathway in this statuary garden. Ali held Sadie by the hand, but Andrew couldn't contain his excitement outside and began running ahead on the path.

"Wow! Look at those huge horns," exclaimed Andrew, who had finally stopped to touch the gigantic tooth protruding from a creature resembling an elephant.

"Not horns, tusks." Said Donnie. "It's a tooth. The mastodons were ancient relatives of our elephants, and they used their tusks both for defense and for digging through the jungle. Like modern elephants, whoever had the best tusks could be the leader of the family. Try to imagine that this whole area was once a huge jungle, with lots of water and marshy plants. There would have been lots of good grass for elephants to eat, and they ate a lot 'cause they were so big. The animals must have been surprised when they got stuck in the sticky tar."

The cement walkways were designed to take guests through the park, through multiple statues of animals, and then back into the main educational part of the museum. Exhibits told the story of living and dying so long ago and the children were somber. Andrew touched the bronze teeth on the dire wolf statue.

"Glad we don't have any of these guys anymore," said Andrew. "Do we have any regular wolfs back home?" "Wolves," corrected Val. "Settlers hunted them all away a long time ago. But you have heard the call of a coyote a few times back at our home. Coyotes are everywhere."

"And I've seen reports of a new creature," said Donnie. "They're calling it a Coy-wolf. It's a new breed of animal, a cross between a wolf and a coyote. Somehow the coyotes have bred with wolves far north of Illinois, even in Canada. The new species has the jaw and teeth of a wolf, but is only a little larger than a coyote. And they're very smart. They are 'urban' animals now."

"What do you mean?" asked Ali.

"This new hybrid is only seen around big cities. They seem to use roads and train tracks to get where they're going. They've been known to steal puppies from domestic mother dogs. Even bring the puppies human dog toys to play with. Kinda weird. But it's evolution happening before our eyes."

"Look at me, Daddy," called Andrew. He was snuggled under the bronze statue of a standing giant ground sloth. The hairy arms looked like they had captured the little boy, and Andrew made a face of fear. Val took several pictures before Sadie joined the fun. She was too little to seem trapped, so instead she reached up to shake hands. Everyone laughed.

Val and Donnie walked the kids all around the park, while Ali took lots of photos for the memory album they would put together when they got home. The kids made the park more interactive than the museum planners could have expected. They climbed on the statues, made faces of terror and fear. Sadie even planted a big kiss on one mastodon tusk. The sun was bright and as the adults were looking around to see what's next, Andrew stuck a finger into a puddle of tar. Sure enough, he couldn't resist touching the black gooey asphalt.

"Guess we have to leave him here," said Val with an exaggerated hysteria in her voice. "We can't have sticky tar in Aunt Ali's car! Did you get it on your shoes?"

"Sorry," said Andrew. "I just had to touch it."

"We know son," said Donnie. "Just be glad the rest of your body stayed on the sidewalk. I guess it's time to go."

"Awww, I'm sorry," said Andrew. "I don't want to leave yet."

"Dumb brother," said Sadie.

The family took one last trip through the gift shop where Ali bought a jigsaw puzzle for a memento of their trip. "Five hundred pieces should keep them busy, plus these coloring books. I'll buy extra for use on the plane trip home. Let's stop for burgers on the way to Ali's. We don't need her to be cooking for us."

"Sounds good," said Ali. "Angus will be dropping over later this afternoon, and you have an early flight tomorrow. I'll take you to my favorite burger joint."

"Thanks for bringing us here, Aunt Ali," said Andrew. "We had fun today and I'll never forget it."

Sadie said, "I'm glad we don't have that sticky tar by our house back home. The bunnies would sure get caught."

The trip to the Tar Pits was one that Donnie especially liked. There were no roller coasters or spinning tea-cups, and he looked forward to a calm afternoon at Ali's apartment pool.

2 5

Back at the apartment, the family spent several hours in the apartment pool. The kids played "Marco Polo" with their dad while Val lounged on a chaise working on a suntan. As the afternoon sun began to dip, they went back to the apartment to rest. Ali made a big batch of popcorn and sat the kids at a small table in the back bedroom. This would give the adults time to talk, and she was concerned enough about what she and Angus had decided to do. She could only hope that Donnie would take it without causing an uproar.

"I'll be ordering pizza for later, but you guys can play in here while the grown-ups talk."

"Can we have pineapple on the pizza?" asked Andrew. "Wasn't I a good kid at the tar pits?"

Ali smiled, "I guess you were. I know you just had to stick a finger in that tar. I'll see what toppings everyone wants. Stay here and play until we call you." She then left the kids to their assignment of leaving the adults alone.

Happily, the kids attacked the coloring books with crayons and markers. Soon colorful pages of mastodons and giant ground sloths abounded. Sadie carefully stayed within the lines while Andrew drew a mustache on the Smilodon. After they'd colored every page, Andrew attacked the jigsaw puzzle by dumping the pieces in a noisy crescendo onto the table. Pieces flew everywhere and though it made Sadie laugh, Andrew's ulterior motives were at play. The puzzle easily kept them occupied while they waited for pizza.

The adults, seated in the living room, heard Angus knock at the door. He came in with stacks of folders under one arm and a bottle of scotch in his hand, nearly spilling papers as he entered. "Hope I'm not a bit too early . . . wanted have time to go over some research afore you all leave." Dressed in his Harris tweed jacket, tartan tie as usual, he looked ready for business.

"Glad to see you, Sir," said Donnie. "Looks like you want my opinion on something?"

"Aye. I've compiled all this research on that princess named Scota, and have something amazing to show you. But you'd best sit doon and get comfortable so I can pass this along to you."

Donnie and Valerie sat down together on the couch while Ali moved a chair close to them for Angus. She stood nearby, then retrieved a tall mailing tube that had been standing in a corner. She passed the tube to Angus. Ominous quiet filled their eyes. They looked serious.

Ali stood like a soldier while Angus spoke. "We've been trying to come up with a way to show this to you, and just couldn't do it long distance." He gently unscrewed the top of the tube.

Ali sighed and started the discussion. "You've never asked, either of you, about how we managed to find you in Gibraltar. Haven't you wondered about it? Or did you think we just got lucky?"

"Of course. I've wondered. I just thought you must have traced my passport or something," Donnie said.

"Your passport was lost, Brother mine. No one knew who you were in the hospital, either. It wasn't just luck."

Donnie was quiet, as if waiting for the sky to open. He had no idea what his sister was up to, and sat farther back into the couch cushions. Val looked at Donnie, almost expecting him to explain it, but of course he never knew how they'd found him. There was nothing he could say about it. In Val's mind, it was just a miracle Donnie had been found, so she never questioned it beyond that. When she first met him in Spain, she didn't realize he was recovering from nearly drowning. But it had been love at first sight, which had only grown stronger over the years.

"We found you because you'd sent me a present from some island off the coast of Gibraltar. We traced the postmark, and with that, tracked you down. Angus was a great detective, and together we were able to find you. The police were helpful also, as the sergeant remembered a 'John Doe' they'd taken to hospital. At the hospital they'd labeled you 'Jerry Flotsam' 'cause you sounded like an American."

"I sent something? What did I send you?" asked Donnie. "I don't remember anything about this time of my life. The doctors have all told me the memories are not accessible due to the near drowning."

Angus nodded and gingerly tapped out the contents of the tube. A piece of yellowed paper was wrapped around what looked like ancient papyrus wrapped in plastic. Angus placed the yellow paper on Donnie's lap. Almost magically, the paper unfurled for Donnie to read it.

Donnie looked down and saw rows of hieroglyphics. His eyes widened as he saw his own handwriting under line after line of glyphs. He started to read, then his eyes scanned the paper. A cartouche circled the name Scota, showing that it was a royal name. Donnie's mouth dropped open as his eyes closed tight. His world went black as he slumped forward in a faint.

Valerie caught him and instantly tried to prop him up. He seemed lifeless. "Donnie, Donnie" she called, but her husband was in a stupor. Angus reached over, took the paper off Donnie's lap, and laid him gently on his back. Ali went to the kitchen for a glass of water and a damp cloth. Donnie had fainted from shock as she expected, but could they bring him back to consciousness or would it be serious like in that hospital? The doctors in Gibraltar had told them Donnie had been unconscious for months and when he finally awoke, Donnie didn't even remember his own name. Ali shook off that thought as Val furiously rubbed her husband's arms, patted his chest. Yes, he was still breathing.

Swimming in blackness, Donnie imagined he was in a pit of black tar. What seemed like lifeless animals pressed against his struggles. He fought to find daylight but could see nothing but blackness because he couldn't open his eyes. They were glued shut in the tar, safely closing him from the outside world. Then, he thought he heard his wife calling, from very far away. He strained to turn his face to that sound, opened his mouth, and formed her name. Tar threatened to clog his own gravelly voice. He heard himself cry "Vaaal."

Donnie's eyes fluttered open and he looked around at his concerned family. "What happened?"

"I'm here, darling. You fainted. Are you all right?" Val stroked his forehead with the damp cloth.

"We showed you your translation that you sent to me so long ago," said Ali. "It was a shock. Remember what we showed you? There's more, though. This will fill in the pieces of the puzzle." She motioned to Angus who delicately lifted the plastic away from the papyrus. The papyrus scrap was damaged in places, but still held together well enough to open.

Angus gingerly began to unroll the papyrus, just enough to show Donnie that it was legit. He spoke not a word, but looked kindly at Donnie, as if to say he was there for support.

"How did you get this?" came the halting words. "I sent this to you? From where? This is illegal!" Donnie's face contorted in denial. He shook his head, trying to disbelieve what was before him. "I cannot have done this for no reason. . . I must have wanted to keep it safe. But from who?"

"We don't know," said Angus, "but you must have sent it before the near drowning. You protected it the best way you could, by sending it to Ali. It came with a package of bath salts, and with that label we found the island and shop where you had bought the stuff. Somehow you sent it to the states for safe keeping. Ali knew something was wrong, since it wasn't her birthday or anything, and when she opened it, she saw that it was an Egyptian relic. That's when she contacted me, and I told her how to take care of it."

"I wanted to turn it into the authorities. But Ali talked me into waiting until we could find you, hopin' you'd explain it. You know the rest, we hid it from you, and the world. Until now. Thought someone was after you. But you seemed safe. Noow, we have to put the pieces right, so you can truly move forward."

Still in shock, Donnie gasped as if he'd been hit by a great block of stone. He felt pressure on his chest. His mind was frozen in disbelief. Then he shook his shoulders as if to shake off the terrible weight. Finally, his legs jerked as if he could force life back into his muscles. As the others watched, he eventually softened and asked to see the papyrus again. As he read through the short passage, rage rose in his chest. As he looked at Angus, more realization of the entirety of it all came through. Donnie choked and coughed as if his throat would seize up. He started to yell, but Val threw herself around his neck and kissed his ear to try to calm him. The scene would have been terrible for the children, to see their father so distraught.

Val's efforts to calm the situation were working, and Donnie cleared his throat. But you could hear the agony in his voice. It seemed a betrayal by his sister, and the friendship he thought he had with Angus. He felt like a patsy, or some fool being guided by Angus, always bugging him about that lost princess. He regained his composure, but not the feeling of safe harbor he'd always had with his family.

"How could you keep this from me?! This blockage has caused me so much misery, so much time lost! My nightmares, my suffering! Why didn't you show this to me right away?"

"Donnie, you were so fragile, we thought it would send you right back into oblivion." Ali expected Donnie to be upset, but she didn't expect him to lash out at her. Or at Angus. "We knew this was illegal, like grave robbing. But there was no way to know where it came from, it was a dead end. Please forgive me." Ali began to cry quietly, and Angus bent closer to Donnie and put his hands on Donnie's knees, trying to re-assert their friendship.

"We half expected you to remember what you were doing in Spain. And all the times I asked you to look for the name of Scota, I expected it to jog your memory. Still nothing?"

"No," Donnie replied tersely. "I can't understand why I would have stolen this important artifact, unless maybe my life was in the balance. What else do you guys know that you aren't telling me?"

Ali wiped tears from her face and began to talk quietly. "It's my fault, really. I refused to let Angus reveal the papyrus, thinking I could protect you. And it's my fault for criticizing that girlfriend you had. Her name was Kemi. You were totally infatuated, I guess. You worked for some outfit called 'Finders, Keepers' whose slogan was, 'we find it, you keep it'."

Donnie was speechless. "I don't remember any of that stuff. Are you making it up?"

"No, it's the truth. I think at that time, with no colleges wanting you, that you just flipped a coin and got in with bad people. It's my fault 'cause I couldn't talk you out of it. I tried really hard, but you wanted to go on digs, no matter what. I'm sorry."

Donnie looked at his sister. Val was still hugging him, and finally said, "If that's what happened, it's not your fault, don't even say that. I know you are honest. I didn't marry a thief!" Then she looked at Angus, and all could tell she wasn't angry at Angus, either.

"This proves your research, Angus," Donnie added. "This is historical proof of those myths. Scotland is named after an Egyptian princess! You're telling me that this was found in Spain, but where? Oh! This is proof of those 'invasion myths' you've told me about. But I'm in big trouble to have done this. If this comes out, I'll be disbarred from my field. What should I do?"

"We won't do anything right now," said Angus. "I'll inquire along some official lines before we do anything. For right now, this is the source of your night terrors, maybe your medical records will support that. You did this thing... for a good reason, maybe to save your life? No one can blame you if your life was in danger, and I think it surely was. Ali and I knew we had to relieve you of this secret. We've kept it from you until we thought you could handle it. We wanted to do it in person. Hope we were right?"

Donnie nodded calmly, then shook his head. *The doctor had been right, even with not knowing what he could have done. Someone tried to murder me, but who? What could I have done to deserve that? And now my reputation, my credibility...everything is in jeopardy.* For some moments, Donnie froze again, then thought back to the Dr. Cohen's prompts. *You screwed up big time, buddy, but you tried to make it right. Say it out loud, "I'm sorry, so sorry."*

Then deeper realizations hit Donnie. He felt like a metal ball in a Newton's Cradle toy, as one ball hit, another ball reacted. His mind slammed from one thought to another, back and forth, clickety clack. Seconds passed and everyone was looking at Donnie, expectantly.

"Gosh, I'm sorry. Sorry I yelled at you guys. I think I understand, and it certainly wasn't your fault. Now that I think about it, waiting to show me this now was really perfect timing. Without the new shrink I have, I wouldn't have believed you today, at all." He clenched his hands and forcibly said, "I'm SORRY!"

Everyone was relieved to see that Donnie had calmed down. Ali laughed out loud. "To think it could have been this easy!" She clapped her hands and went to the phone to order pizza. Donnie just stared at her. *She thinks this is all over? This is not fixed!*

Val sat hugging Donnie, not saying anything. She realized the jeopardy better than Ali, and had seen Donnie struggle so long with the nightmares. His position at work, and the quagmire of what to do next were racing through her mind. But it was not over by a long shot.

Angus loosened his tie, and went to get glasses and the bottle. "This calls for a toast," he said with a smile, "Noow we can move forward at last." He carefully re-wrapped the papyrus and inserted it back into the tube. "I'll keep it safe for now," said Angus, "but here, have a copy of the glyphs and translation. Sure, there's more work to do, but *dinna fasch*." Then he added emphatically, "I promise nothing will happen to you, and I won't involve your sister. You are not to worry. I think 'tis best to turn it in anonymously. You won't get credit for the find, neither will I. Then we'll just research the hell out of it."

Donnie sighed deeply and took another look at his translation. The yellowed paper had some crossed-out words and corrections, but all in all it read smoothly. An Egyptian princess had once lived in Spain. Then his brain comfortably flipped into research mode.

"The language is more archaic than I'd expect if it was from the thirtieth dynasty era." Donnie showed a couple of phrases to Angus, who had returned with the bottle. Angus nodded in agreement.

"That's one of the problems I saw, too." replied the Scot. The professor had studied the papyrus at leisure, while Donnie had only scanned the short page. "We'd no expect that particular glyph, especially here, and here again.." He pointed an arthritic finger at several spots, emphasizing the problem.

"I see a few more examples, and this turn of phrase. What does this mean?" Donnie asked as he reached for blank paper that Ali had left next to the couch. He sketched out a few glyphs as they sat head-to-head discussing the various glyphs. Then Angus referenced other research Donnie might know about.

"Maybe this is more evidence of what Krauss was finding in his research. And even Pruesinszky? If Ramses II dates are wrong, why not those of Nectanebus in the Thirtieth?"

"There's another problem too," added Donnie, ". . . with the nicknames you sent me to find. I found one instance where Ramses III used the same festival gnomon as one used later by Nectanebus II. And the avenue of human-headed sphinxes was supposedly built by three pharaohs in succession. Maybe it was just one? I always thought it was odd that it would have taken such a huge span of centuries to complete."

"We have a major concurrence with this papyrus, but no way to publish it," said Angus. "We'll just have to keep looking for correlations, hope to find other cultural connections. Eventually something will turn up. Who knows, maybe they'll find more mummies."

Donnie chuckled, "Well, legends say Nectanebus II became a fortune teller in some bazaar in Macedonia. Good luck with that." Then he asked, "Have you had the papyrus tested? Radiocarbon? What was obtained?"

"You know as well as I there's a window of plus or minus hundreds of years. It doesn't help. But we got dates of both 1250's or 300's. Too much of a discrepancy. Just like the tiles at Medinet Habu. Linguistically we may have a better handle on it, after this find is published. The problems aren't going away, and if it takes the rest of my life, I'll crack it!"

"Another weird connection happened last week," Angus added. "They've just uncovered an entire bull's remains buried in Ramses II's temple at Abydos. What's more, in several niches there they found twelve votive bulls' heads and bones dated from Ptolemaic times. Which leads us to believe that the more recent Egyptians kept the old rituals going. For a thousand years? It's hard to fathom, since by then religion should have changed so much."

Donnie nodded and said, "Sure, conventional belief is that that form of bull worship had died out way before the Ptolemies. Did the Egyptians revere Ramses II after such an immense span of time? Still, by the time of the Ptolemies not many could read the glyphs. I wonder why they were still interring bulls. Go figure."

Occasionally the men would glance up and see the women standing there, watching, but Angus kept the discussion on details, trying his best to keep Donnie from his personal involvement. Their search for validation had become almost an addiction, the nuances of ancient glyphs their opiate. The men were obsessed with the sticky tangents of chronology, but eventually Donnie rebelled.

"The truth is, I hate my job," he muttered to Angus. "I like to dig, and research. But not publish. I can't take much more from my department. I thought all my life would be happy getting to be a professor. But no. I need to come clean about this theft."

"It's the honorable thing to do, Laddie. But your family? Don't rush into jeopardy!"

Donnie nodded, "I'll do what's best. Talk with Val first. We have a long plane flight but I'll figure out what to do by next week. You let the papyrus be found."

Angus felt proud of Donnie, as if he were the son he never had. "Sure, 'tis right, Don. Don't act in haste. It goes with a fall, as my mum would say. Use your wits and we'll make it oot alright. Proud o'you."

Out of earshot, the ladies were in the kitchen. Val looked at Ali, who seemed to ignore the ramifications. She was humming some tune, totally pleased with the outcome. As if to her the problem was already resolved. The apartment was subdued, but occasionally they'd hear laughter from the kids' area. The pizza would arrive very soon.

"What do you think they'll do?" Val asked. She hesitated to bring in the kids.

"Well, the papyrus was taken and sent to me outside the rules of archaeology... You're trained, you should know," said Ali flippantly. "I'm just glad the secret is out, and I don't feel guilty about keeping it from you anymore. I trust Angus to be careful, it's not only Donnie's reputation, but his, too."

157

"Yes, I understand that," Val said, "but there's a different problem. I know Donnie's been hammering against the established chronology. If they use the papyrus to support their claims, those men will drive him out! His department is nothing but conservative."

"Give it time. Angus and I have waited seven years, you know. Maybe they can contain their enthusiasm until they find other evidence. Angus will be super careful."

"That might not be enough. Guess I'd rather this papyrus had been lost in the mail!"

Val got up and went to check on the kids. The jigsaw puzzle was almost done, but several holes were missing where the mastodon tusks should be. Sadie had left the table and was sitting by herself.

"Andrew is hiding pieces," complained Sadie. "He always wants to be the winner!"

Andrew began to look around on the floor and "found" the last piece. But Val gave him a stern look. He knew he'd been caught.

"Go wash your hands Sadie, please," said her mother. "Pizza will soon be here. When it comes, Andrew will be in here putting the puzzle away and straightening up the room." Val directed a stern and impatient gaze at her son. Sadie smiled, and skipped to the kitchen. Andrew sat with egg on his face.

"We'll have a little talk, later," Val said. Then she went to rejoin the adults in the living room. The men were still involved in animated conversation and Donnie drew more glyphs. Angus smiled in camaraderie. They looked like teenagers swapping Dungeon and Dragons cards, gleefully rearranging words and discerning more clues. When the doorbell rang with the pizza delivery, neither man even noticed the sound, so intent were they with their discussion.

Ali and Val arranged plates and napkins in the dining area, Sadie came to help. Everyone grabbed a slice of pizza quickly, it smelled so good. Val went to fetch Andrew who saw that they hadn't eaten every slice. He quickly joined in the feast. An excellent Scottish Ale was poured for toasts, much to Angus' enjoyment. The kids had sodas. Eventually all the pizza disappeared, and Ali came out of the kitchen with a big chocolate cake for dessert. After setting down some plates for the cake she returned to the kitchen and brought out some excellent Scotch which Angus held up for a toast. "All for one, and one for all," he joked. "Really, though we are four. We've been victorious tonight!"

Sadie and Andrew had quizzical looks on their faces. Weren't there six of them? Donnie explained, "Angus is talking about the Three Musketeers, who were great French soldiers. But Aunt Ali has helped me with big problems, not to mention a great vacation for our family. Maybe you kids should call our friend "Uncle Angus" from now on, as he's part of our family too."

Sadie and Andrew nodded in agreement while Angus smiled broadly. "Your Daddy and I make a good team for sure. Thanks for including me in the family. *Scots wha hae!*"

26

Back at home in Illinois, Donnie was working in his study area. On one hand he had a stack of research from Angus about correcting the accepted Egyptian chronology from the 20th to the 30th dynasties. In the pile there were records from Hittites, as well as Greek historians like Strabo, Thucydides, and Herodotus. So many modern researchers had discounted their histories, but as time passed, modern technologies agreed the old histories were more than fables. For instance, before photography was invented, tourist sketches showed four pyramids on the Giza plateau. Only the head of the Great Sphinx protruded from the sand. Modern Egyptians, unable to read hieroglyphics, saw only useful building blocks, and evidently dismantled the fourth smaller pyramid. Whose monument it was or where the blocks went, archaeologists and historians will never know. *The honest history just gets remade to fit by someone with power.*

Herodotus also wrote about a waterway for boats to sail up to the pyramids, and said dignitaries could sail around the Great Sphynx, in great celebrations. Studies of the erosion calculated by geologists had since proven this to be correct. Fourteenth century visitors didn't even know the Sphynx was there until the sand below the head was removed, thus revealing the huge body of a lion. *Few people believe Herodotus was accurate,* thought Donnie.

One stack of papers on Donnie's desk had sticky tabs hanging out that looked like little pink stepping stones. But they were going nowhere. The pile spoke of the complicated legend of an unknown princess nicknamed Scota. No mention of her could be cross-referenced with any artifacts yet found, except for the stolen papyrus. Donnie was at an impasse, and his career was on the line if theft was involved in finding it. But if Angus could have its authenticity documented and somehow "find it" in the university's extensive artifact collection, then he could claim the find as his own. UCLA probably has a good quantity of mis-labeled material stuck in some musty drawer. There must be other material with incomplete provenance waiting to be found. It would be perfectly fitting for a Scottish Egyptologist to find it, and take credit for it. *Works for me. Why not just let Angus pursue it?*

To the right side of his laptop, Donnie had another stack of papers and books. There were several copies of Homer's *Iliad* and *Odyssey*, even CliffsNotes, and a rough outline of the hero's travels homeward. Even more perturbing were other archaeological records about an ancient city named Troia, which once thrived on the westernmost coast of Iberia. Somewhere beneath Lisbon, Portugal, were the ruins of an ancient harbor. Archaeologists found remains of a massive trading center which had been consumed by both a war and the ocean. The coastline which had once held an expansive peninsula, had submerged. Greek historians told of earthquakes, crushing waves, and pillaging, which ended civilization there. But which era? The Sea Peoples' raids in the Mediterranean could be placed around 1200 BCE, which would coincide with the destruction of Wilusa in the eastern Mediterranean. But this was only conjecture. Donnie was at a serious juncture.

Val was in the kitchen fixing macaroni and cheese for the kids. Lunch was easily made for they weren't picky eaters. Donnie and Val would have leftovers of some cold fried chicken. But there was lots of work waiting in the backyard, as a herd of rabbits had demolished their little garden plot while they were in California. Nothing remained above ground and there were more than a few holes under the fence for bunnies to come and go. Donnie had bought some extra tall garden edging at a garden store, and planned to add it to the base of the picket fencing when he had time. Unless that worked, their home garden would continue to be preyed upon by prairie critters.

Val fixed a plate of chicken for Donnie and brought it to him. He was sitting at his computer but the screen was blank.

"Did you run out of words?" she asked.

"Worse than that," came Donnie's soft voice. "I don't know which pile to work on anymore. Toss a coin?"

Val kissed her husband's neck. "What's the best use of your time? Don't you have other stuff to do before the semester starts up?" Donnie didn't answer.

"Can I help? Maybe let's have lunch first and we can talk about it?"

Donnie closed the laptop and nodded. The computer's black top peered up at him like a cavernous, bottomless pit. The heat of the summer seemed to have fried Donnie's brain, and the two stacks of papers were constantly at war with one another. He felt as if he were constantly running the gauntlet between them.

"I'd love to have your input," he said to Val, "'cause I can't choose. Maybe if I believed the book would sell for more than a 'dollar two ninety' I'd have more faith in it. The work with Angus is even more precarious, you know."

"What can you tell me about your Bronze age pirates?"

"You know civilization came to a standstill all over the Mediterranean, all the great cities crumbled to dust. Seemed like a sudden collapse, and even the religions changed from worshipping Goddesses to male figures. Maybe the pirates just terrorized everything and the goddesses didn't protect anymore. Plus, I think the battles also happened in the Atlantic too."

"I can see that, kinda like the Norse cultures expanded then, too. The whole world changed. Warring people came down from the north, we have their weapons to prove it. Of course, that would have been much earlier," said Val.

"If I can show that the Trojan war happened in the Atlantic instead, it will really piss off the department. But I can't ignore the ancient myths that say a major war happened on the west coast of Iberia. Later, the ancient city was called 'Alis Ubbo' which meant 'born of Ulysses.' It had been on a peninsula that fell beneath the sea. It was destroyed in one day, like from an earthquake or tsunami. We know the Sea Peoples were sacking all the cities in the Mediterranean, the Egyptians won the major battle. But the widespread climate destruction would have made all those cities easy pickings."

"Aren't there Norse myths, too?" asked Val.

"There is an Eddic poem that tells about a famous hero named Ullr who was the son of the goddess Sif. Maybe the stranger known as Homer heard those tales and transformed the story into Greek heroes. The toponomy of the north Atlantic still has names like Ullapool, Ullswater, and something called the Ulster Cycle. We just need to not confuse the various myths about worldwide floods, like Gilgamesh and the creation stories of Enki into one big catastrophe. There must have been many caught in the racial memory."

Donnie's mind raced. *If the Battle of Troy was actually fought on Atlantic shores, it would be more likely to hear crashing waves. And the extended shoreline could hold thousands of ships. Plus, "sailing for nine days without sight of land" would be unlikely in the Aegean. The whirlpool of Corryvreckan is a perfect Charybdis, while the Sirens singing is really the extended hours of singing done by women waulking the wool. I don't believe in one-eyed giants, but goat and sheep herds were important industries there too.*

Val nodded, understanding the complexity of the problem. "Let's have some lunch. We can ponder over some cold fried chicken. I'll break open some beer and let the kids eat outside."

So, they retreated to the shaded back porch. The kids played on the swing-set after eating, oblivious to the hot rays of the Illinois sun. Donnie and Val relaxed, just like old times. Donnie felt his future was at a crossroads. He still hadn't fully recovered from the shock he endured at Ali's house. Now he struggled to get the words out, but then he took the plunge. "Val, I don't want to go back to the U. I'm sick of the stress there." He felt the words hanging in the hot air, and waited for them to hit the ground.

Val nearly choked mid-swallow. "Okay…umm, what?"

"On the plane I gave it lots of thought. There's other work I can do. Those stuffed shirts don't care about real research, or truth. They ignore me when I'm there, or even if I pass by in the break room, they do their best to avoid me. I feel like it's only a matter of time 'til they get enough reason to strip away my position. We've never been invited to anyone's house, have we?"

"Nope, you're right. I just thought it was because we have young kids, and your colleagues are all so old. I haven't got much in common with any of the wives I've met. I just ignored it, but didn't know how bad it was for you at work. What ideas do you have?"

"Out of the blue one of my mentors at BU sent my credentials to a group in Britain who were looking for good field researchers. He always said I should stay in the dirt, but he knew I'd be interested in authenticating provenance on stuff being sold. Anyway, I followed up on it, it's a good position with the British Museum. They have an on-line platform where I could focus on artifacts stolen from Egypt and Sudan. It's called CircArts. They're funded by their Cultural Protection Fund, and evidently pay even better than what I'm getting now. Seems like what I should do." Donnie paused and looked at Val. She wasn't showing signs of shock! Her face was open and she was listening.

"Plus, I'd like to get a detective interested in that company 'Finders, Keepers'. Seems to me they tried to kill me. I may be a risk-taker, but I can't believe I'd jump off a boat so far off shore. Even as a dare. They might have thought they'd get rid of me. Didn't know I could swim to Gibraltar."

"Donnie, I know you! You wouldn't be involved with looting artifacts! You are too trusting. They probably scored lots of money with you being the finder. I'd bet anything they tried to eliminate you somehow. I'm with you all the way on that."

"Remember when we were at that shop in Disneyland? I thought some of that stuff looked suspicious, I mean museum quality artifacts being sold like that. Guess I'm not happy with what was being sold there, but I instantly thought they might be looted."

Val shook her head. "No, you're right! I thought so too! Let's go for it!"

Donnie embraced his wonderful wife, content in knowing they would get through this together. He felt it was the right thing to do, and with her full support, they'd get justice.

"The CircArts organization seems to have deep pockets and lots of investigators. We could be a team."

"That's a brilliant idea!" Val clapped her hands with glee. "Let's track thieves of artifacts. Yes, apply right away! You'd be great at that, and Dr. Sturm can go to Hell!"

Val then added, "Even if they won't take us both, maybe we could move?"

"Where would you like to go? We've got the kids to think about. Are you worried, at all?"

"Nope! Our kids are young. It's not like uprooting them outta high school. Let's go west. You know I have an adventurous spirit… you shoulda known that when I went off with you in Spain! Let's find more Norse stuff. It must continue across the continent, and you could find it. And as far as looted artifacts, the Southwest is rife with pottery thieves. There's controversy in New Mexico, lots of pottery thefts, and who knows what you'll find. You are the best finder! And it would be great to catch some artifact thieves. I might have told you there was pressure on me when I was an intern. Remember?"

"Seems like you felt someone was following you, or upset because you suspected they were fencing some artifacts on the side?"

"Yeah, but I had no proof. Things there were just a little suspicious. I wasn't even sure they put the Roman coins you found back on display. I thought they got sold off somehow. Anyway, there was an undercurrent of some sort of illegal trade. We'd both be good at that kind of detective work."

Val squeezed Donnie's hand, gave him a kiss on the cheek, and made him know for sure that she was with him all the way. Donnie wasn't the only one sick of Illinois.

Donnie could hardly believe his ears. This wonderful lady, true to her nature, was as adventurous as he was. They had always made a great team. They both just sat on the porch swing, in perfect unison, thinking about a bright future within their grasp.

"Send in updated resumes with a really good letter of interest. If there's any justice in the world, they'll be happy to have us on their team. I think this will work!" The idea was such a happy thought for Val, somehow it seemed like fate was on their side this time.

"Like you said before, 'we have the creds.' The Brits are looking for a good team. I'm so glad you're on board with this plan. I'll keep writing this novel, too. We should get an answer pretty quick, since this job just opened up."

"Yeah, your book should sell easily. I know we can self-publish it cheaply, and the department can't complain about fiction. Can they?"

"I guess not. But Angus might be miffed if I put him off even longer. He's waited a long time to publish his love affair with Scota. You know she is the goddess who keeps her shield erected to separate our world from the world of the dead. Or should I say, the 'ever young.' It's important to us Scots, somehow in my DNA too. It's like those in the Otherworld are just watching us, waiting for us to get things right. I just think I can't do both projects right now. I want to concentrate on getting a different job."

"I'm not scared." said Val. "I think you should just concentrate on the novel, see how fast it comes together. Who knows, maybe this is an open door, and we should give it a try."

The porch swing moved ever so slowly as Val and Donnie watched the kids play in the yard. Andrew had one electric car going under the arc of the swing while Sadie was swinging over it. She was carefully lifting her legs so to miss the little sports car. The grass was too high anywhere else in the yard for the car except for under the swings where there was dirt. As usual, he was having fun teasing his sister. As Donnie watched his kids, internally he knew it was time to move.

Val kept holding his hand. This was the man she had chosen long ago in Spain. His courage, his honesty, his intellect, he still shone like a star in her eyes. She would follow him anywhere, and the kids were young enough to see it as an adventure. Wherever they would go, it would be a new experience, and Donnie would find the best place for them all to grow. She knew he was the kind of guy that wanted to go against accepted evidence and look for other angles or ways of looking at the past.

Donnie had worked so hard to get his position in academia, only to find it wasn't the place for him. He needed field work, or at least detective work on artifacts. Getting away made sense. Donnie would write the novel and prove that Ulysses, the greatest archer of all the Isles, fought in the north Atlantic. His strong arm would have snapped the puny bows depicted at Medinet Habu.

"There's something else," Donnie mumbled. "Something I hadn't thought about before. Dr. Cohen mentioned there's a connection between blood types and behaviors."

"What?" asked Val. She had no idea where this idea was going.

"Evidently people like us, with Rh-negative blood, are statistically more prone to car accidents. I know we haven't had any, but she just meant that we are risk-takers. It's funny, but I think most wives would have talked me out of the harebrained idea about changing careers. Seems like it doesn't even faze you."

Val was quiet, trying to understand what Donnie was saying. "Why should blood type have an effect on behavior? That's silly."

"Well, there's a parasite called Toxoplasmosis that causes antigens in the human brain. Because all humans have been exposed to this pathogen for millions of years, people have this antigen that protects them from the parasite. Except Rh-negative people. Us. Somehow, over thousands of years, our blood type wasn't exposed to cats. And cats were everywhere. Remember they found them at the tar pits?"

"You're telling me that's why I don't like cats?"

"No, worse than that. Our blood type people must have lived where there were no cats. There's no such place on Earth, now, at least above water."

"Oh, so we're aliens?"

"Right," said Donnie sarcastically. "I'm not that wacko. No, I meant whatever land mass where the people lived must have been isolated from the rest of human population for at least twenty thousand years. Wherever that was, it's not here anymore."

"It's hard for me to believe some antigen makes me adventurous," said Val.

"But I've been reading a lot about how different bacteria affect the brain. Have you heard about the latest Autism studies with mice?" As they sat on the shady porch swing, Donnie explained how researchers had developed bacteria-free mice. These little animals could be exposed to certain strains of bacteria which seemed to alter the normal behaviors of the mice. By taking gut bacteria from an obese human, and infecting the mice with it, scientists could generate fat mice even without adding to their caloric intake. Somehow the bacteria caused the mice to gain weight.

Val nodded, but kept listening.

"Another experiment showed how mice could lose their physical ability of walking balanced on a wooden plank. By exposing them to gut bacteria from a Parkinson's patient, the mice could no longer walk the plank with good balance. The difference was measurable. The third experiment investigated Autism, and the behavior of repeated, even uncontrollable repetitive movements. The scientists put black marbles perfectly spaced in rows, on top of the cage litter. After exposing them to the gut bacteria from an autistic person, the mice repeatedly tried to cover up the marbles with litter. They did this until they were exhausted, as if the black marbles were a threat to their lives. Somehow the various bacterial fauna had an effect on behaviors of previously healthy mice."

Val listened quietly, thinking about Andrew being so overly active. Donnie thought about all the risks he had taken throughout his life. "Maybe it was a risk I took, even getting on that boat near the coast of Gibraltar."

"We'll never know unless you find those treasure hunters. But knowing you, I think you just tried to do the right thing, 'cause you mailed the papyrus to Ali. That much is clear. But I don't know enough about genetics to understand the cat thing. What's your idea?"

"I think we need to get our DNA done, both of us. Maybe we're part of Haplogroup X after all, and if that's true, I know why I've been so interested in finding out where they came from. They must have come from a land mass that was isolated from cats. And there's no such place in the world today. Lots of island governments have restrictions on importing cats, because the local fauna has no defenses. The cats can eliminate the wildlife. Like lots of bird species are no longer found in the Hawaiian Islands because they've been decimated by feral cats. But I'm talking about some land mass that was isolated twenty million years ago."

"Why twenty million years?" asked Val.

"Because that's when the Rhesus blood types are first detected in homo sapiens' DNA. As humans migrated out of the sub-Sahara, they expanded to all the continents. Even to the South Pacific. Somehow all the branches of human beings intermarried, you know, Neanderthals, Denisovans, etcetera, and those that were exposed to the toxoplasmosis parasite developed antigens. But some people, who are less than ten percent of the human population, were isolated from both cats and the Rhesus factor. They must have lived on an island mass separate from the continents."

"Like Greenland or Iceland?" suggested Val.

"Well, that land mass would have been covered with ice at the last Glacial Maximum. I do think there was other land, somewhere in the Atlantic. I'm no geologist but I've been reading new research that talks about the upward movement of the earth's crust that transformed the Straits of Gibraltar into a dam. Around twenty thousand years ago, the oceans had less water due to glaciers. When the glaciers eventually melted, the sea level rose all over the world. Even paleolithic settlements off the coast of Australia are now under three hundred feet of water. There would have been more ocean cutting off any land in the Atlantic from the European plate, isolating this land mass. We know that the water level in the Mediterranean Sea fluctuated wildly within human history. Structures around the islands of Malta are under nearly three hundred feet of water. Even early Egyptian records describe the water as a great lake, much smaller than a sea. So the Mediterranean used to vary in size, depending on the ice sheets. Anyway, between around five million years and a hundred seventy thousand years ago, the Mediterranean was sealed off by a 'dam' at the Straits of Gibraltar. All this could be stored somehow in human memory."

"Then what happened?"

"The African Plate subducted under the Eurasian Plate which pulled the entire region downwards. Whatever land mass was west of Gibraltar dropped four-hundred kilometers beneath the water level. A huge deluge then broke through the arc of Gibraltar, refilling the lower land to the east, forming the Mediterranean Sea. It didn't happen overnight, like a huge earthquake, but how fast it happened is hard to tell. I think geologists argue about this all the time."

"Okay, so this land mass either sank or got so small that the people sailed away?"

"That's my idea. Plato states that Atlantis was west of the Pillars of Hercules. If it existed, the sinking would have coincided with the glacier melt around twelve thousand years ago. I always thought he meant the island was in the north Atlantic. But what if it was where he said it was? Within sailing distance to Iberia and north Africa. There is something called the Majuan Ridge underwater there, that could be the remains. The whole area that belongs to Morocco has several islands that are left from the subduction. And that area wouldn't be a too-distant sail to account for the Rh-negative Berbers, Basques, or Canary Islanders. It just makes sense to me that they came from some central location, but close enough to sail to North Africa and Iberia. Some must have gotten farther north to the Hebrides. Plato said Atlantis sank twelve thousand years ago, so putting the clues together it all makes sense. Even the Kennewick Man dates to this period, because the land bridge must have been gone thousands of years before. His skull looks more Ainu than North American Indian. This major sinking might be constrained into the Noah's flood story, rather than just localized flooding. There are over six hundred flood stories, from all over the world. The Rh-negative factor is the best clue. Someday, I'll prove it!"

Val hugged Donnie with all her strength. She was going to support Donnie, no matter what. She believed his hypothesis too, knowing they could research the geology as well as the genetics. She looked Donnie straight in the eyes and said, "I'm with you all the way!"

Inside his head Donnie heard a mental "cheer" of triumph. He jumped from the swing, with Val close behind, and ran to collect the kids. "We're off to the Grady's Family amusement park. And I want a ride on the Tilt-a-Twirl!"

GLOSSARY

Amenti. The Egyptian word for the Otherworld, or Heaven. Only the truth-filled souls are admitted there after the weighing of one's heart.

Bodhrum. A shallow round Scottish drum played by wrist movements, using a 'tipple' rather than drumsticks. The drum has a variety of note progressions depending on what part of the drum head is played.

Brendan Voyage. An adventurous voyage using authentic boat-making skills, historically made by Christian monks. A modern-day man proved that the boats could sail from Britain to Nova Scotia.

Browne, Sir Thomas, MD. 1605-1682 Famous for his scientific thought and letters, numerous quotations and aphorisms attest to his mighty intellect. He is credited with coining dozens of new words such as electricity, computer, hallucination, pathology, ambidextrous, approximate, cryptography, parturition, praying mantis, etc. Credited with being the first to notice that safe things to eat show a five-part pattern when cut open. "Think before you act, think twice before you speak."

Caber. The wooden pole thrown in Celtic competition. The poles are assessed by weight and length, and must be balanced, then thrown end-over-end for the throw to count.

Coracle. Small round or very broad boat made of wickerwork and interwoven laths, covered with waterproof layers of animal skins, tanned or oiled cloth. Found in Wales, and other Celtic communities in ancient times in the Hebrides.

dinna fasch a Scottish colloquial idiom meaning "don't worry."

Gàidhlig . The Scottish version of Gaelic, mainly spoken in the Highlands or Hebridean Islands of Scotland.

Heiros ganos. Sacred marriage of a mortal man with a goddess.

Hittites. Bronze age culture east and north of Egypt, the source of many wars and alliances of ancient Mediterranean peoples.

Hisarlik. A major city of the Hittites, which some believe was where Troy once stood on the Turkish coast.

Kom Ombo. An unusual temple in Upper Egypt constructed during Ptolemaic Dynasties, 180-47 BCE. Over three hundred crocodile mummies were interred there to honor the crocodile god Sobek.

Medinet Habu. Mortuary temple built by Rameses III near the west bank at Luxor, Egypt. The construction site is supposedly the first place where the god Amun appeared. It is built like a fortress; many murals depict the victory of the pharaoh against the Sea Peoples.

Papyrus. Egyptian paper made from the papyrus reed. Also refers to the document as a whole as the Egyptian library at Alexandria was said to have thousands of books by papyrus.

Reticule. A net bag or string pouch used by Medieval ladies as a purse.

Serk. Or sometimes 'sark', a Broad Scots word for 'shirt' A 'sarkin weaver' could weave a shirt with no seams.

Sgian dubh. Small, short dagger worn in the knee sock of a Scottish man's costume. The knife hilt may be bent slightly near the top and set with a large cabochon stone.

Sporran. A pouch with a flap, usually made of badger fur or other leather, which is worn at the middle front of the man's kilt. It hangs on chains which attach to the belt.

Tartan. Woven wool plaid fabric in specially repeated color sequences related to a surname or Scottish clan. See 'Mummies of Urumchi' for Neolithic samples of the earliest tartans found. The weave is a special 'twill' not generally found outside of Scotland until present times.

Waulking **songs** are simple, rhythmic Scottish folk songs, traditionally sung in the Gaelic language by a group of women, as they beat newly woven wool tweed or tartan cloth against a table to thicken and soften it. Also called fulling, this process is called 'waulking' in Scottish English, from Scots 'waukin.'

FOR FURTHER READING

*The asterisk at the end of Ullyxes' speech is a quotation from "Tain Bo Cuaigne," the Book of Leinster, an oral legend written down by Irish monks in Latin, around 600AD.

Aston, David, Radiocarbon, Wine Jars, and New Kingdom Chronology, 2020

Brice, T., The Kingdom of the Hittites, Oxford U. Press, 2005

Campbell, Joseph, The Masks of God, Oriental Mythology, 1970

Cline, Eric H., 1187 The Year Civilization Collapsed, 2014

Dickenson, O., "The Collapse at the end of the Bronze Age" Oxford handbook of the Bronze Age Aegean, Oxford U. Press, pp 483-490

Drews, Robert, The End of the Bronze Age, 1993

Eisler, Riane, The Chalice and the Blade, 1988

Gertoux, Gerard, "Absolute Egyptian Chronology Based on Synchronisms Dated by Astronomy Versus Carbon 14 Dating"

Ginenthal, Charles, Pillars of the Past Vol. I, II, III, IV, 2015

Govers, et al, "Choking the Mediterranean to Dehydration: The Messinian Salinity Crisis," Geology, 37 (2): 167

James, Peter, Centuries of Darkness, 1991

Johnson, W. Raymond and Heidel, Jay, Secrets of the Stones: Epigraphic Study at Medinet Habu, U. of Manchester, 2001

Kaniewski, D. and Campo, V., "The Sea Peoples from Cuneiform Tablets to Carbon Dating," Academic Search Premier, June 2001

Lambert, Joseph B., Traces of the Past, 1997

Lang, Andrew, Tales of Troy, Ulysses, the Sacker of Cities, 1912

Manning, SW., "Why Radiocarbon dating 1200 BCE is difficult: a sidelight on dating at the end of the Late Bronze Age and the contrarian contribution," Scripta Mediterrania, 2006-007.

MOTA press release, 8 April 2020, "New Discovery of foundation deposits and the storerooms of Reamesses II's temple at Abydos"

Neumann, J., Parpola, S., "Climactic change and the eleventh-tenth century eclipse of Assyria and Babylonia," Journal of Near Eastern Studies, 46: 161-182, 1987

Nyland, Edo, Odysseus and the Sea Peoples, A Bronze History of Scotland, 2001

Onvlee, Ian, "Redating the Early 18th Dynasty," 2013

Oppenheimer, C., Eruptions that Shook the World, 2011

Papers from Langford Conference, Florida University, 2007, "Political Economies of the Aegean Bronze Age"

Romey, Kristin, The Vogelbarke of Medinet Habu, 2003

Science Daily: Scientists Reconstruct What Gibraltar Was Like 9 Million Years Ago, Jan. 27, 2017

Selincourt, Aubrey, The World of Herodotus, 1962

Severin, Tim, The Brendan Voyage, 1988

Utrecht University, "Mediterranean Sea Dried Up Five Million Years Ago," Science Daily, 12 Feb. 2009

Velikovsky, Immanuel, The Sea Peoples, 1997

Velikovsky, Immanuel, Ages in Chaos, 1977

Ward, Cheryl A., "Seafaring in the Bronze Age Aegean: Evidence and Speculation," in Political Economies of the Aegean Bronze Age, pp. 149-160. Oxbow, 2010

Weiss, H., Courty, M.A., Wetterstrom, W., Guichard F., Senior L., et al, "The Genesis and Collapse of Third Millennium North Mesopotamian Civilization," 1993, Science, 261: 995-1004

AFTERWORD

My love of ancient Egypt began at age four, when I taught myself to read Egyptian fables. The forty-two laws of the Goddess Maat have been my guide, and her directive, to "make maat prosper" has caused me to search for the truth within myths. I hope that by revisiting these myths, history will come alive to my readers and the evidence for the historical Scota will someday be revealed.

ABOUT THE AUTHOR

Michele Lang Buchanan grew up in the secret city of Los Alamos, New Mexico, as her father was an early scientist on the Manhattan Project. After earning her Ph.D. at the University of New Mexico, she enjoyed a fulfilling career as a special education teacher for the Albuquerque Public Schools and also at the Juvenile Detention Center, working mostly with Behavior Disordered and other categories of disabled children. After retiring, she delved into playing the Celtic harp, and began performing at local Renfaires and Celtic Festivals. With her costuming skills she provides period garb for the Celtic Singers of New Mexico, and items by request, though she has retired her company called "Affordable Vestments."

Born to teach, Michele delivers lectures on Scottish history, harp history, and many other topics. She lives in Albuquerque with her husband Tom, and enjoys performing harp and vocals for special events, retired veterans, hospice, and retirement homes. As an award-winning fiber artist, her embroidery, quilts, and needlework projects keep her hands busy. It is a love affair with strings!

Made in the USA
Columbia, SC
26 May 2023

17355855R10121